UNDERCOVER LOVERS

UNDERCOVER LOVERS

ANDREW NEIDERMAN

OPEN ROAD

INTEGRATED MEDIA

NEW YORK

ISBN: 978-1-5040-7601-2

This edition published in 2022 by Open Road Integrated Media, Inc.
180 Maiden Lane
New York, NY 10038
www.openroadmedia.com

UNDERCOVER
LOVERS

ANDREW NEIDERMAN

FROM OPEN ROAD MEDIA

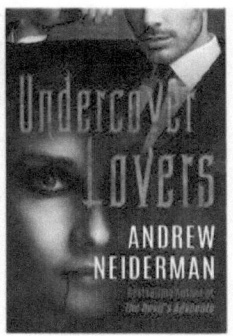

OPEN ROAD

INTEGRATED MEDIA

INTEGRATED MEDIA

Find a full list of our authors and
titles at www.openroadmedia.com

FOLLOW US
@OpenRoadMedia

I wasn't going to Russia or any other country with Franco.

I shoved my hand into my pocket and retrieved my cell phone. I turned it on silent and sent out a text requesting help.

I didn't know how long I had until the flight or until they searched me. I'd been foolish not to bring a knife or, at the very least, mace, some kind of weapon to defend myself.

I had memorized Mason's number, having stalked him online. It had been years since we'd seen each other.

We'd gone to boarding school together. He had joined the army after high school, and I had been sent to live with my father.

It was no secret he worked for the security firm Eagle Tactical. I couldn't call them. It would be too risky.

I hoped that their business line could receive texts. I didn't have Mason's personal number; it appeared to be unlisted.

Mason, I need your help. Please track my phone and come for me. I wouldn't ask if this wasn't life or death— my death. Hazel

It was short and to the point. It was all I could do. I hoped it would go through and he'd come for me.

CHAPTER TWO

ARIELLA

Sunlight filtered in through the skylight casting the kitchen in a warm golden tone.

The aroma of coffee filled the room, and I hurried to the pot, grabbed a cup, and poured myself a drink.

Izzie sat at the kitchen table eating a bowl of cereal. It was the quietest I'd ever seen her, except when she napped.

Jaxson clomped down the stairs, dressed and ready to go.

I still needed to shower, but I'd be quick. "Are we driving into work together?" I asked.

"No." His response was short, his tone cold, emotionless.

Had I done something to piss him off?

We hadn't talked about that night when he'd found me in the shower, curled up with water pounding over me. I'd been unable to move, shaken to the core. He'd dressed me, carried me to bed, and slept beside me.

It was the only night I'd slept in that bedroom. I was now delegated to the guest room, which I guess made sense.

We agreed that if he was going to be my boss, we had to keep things platonic.

That wasn't what I wanted, but I had mixed feelings. He hadn't stuck around after the one night we shared at my place before the fire burned my house to the ground. We also hadn't spoken about it, and now it seemed pointless to rehash a relationship that couldn't ever be.

I stared at him, the cup of coffee poised at my lips, two hands on my mug.

The tremors were under control, and while my house had burned down, I was able to get a prescription from the local doctor for the medications I needed for my battle with autonomic dysfunction. I was managing for the most part.

His cell phone rang and he grabbed it off the kitchen counter.

"Morning, Declan. What's up?" He waltzed into the living room for privacy, at least some semblance of it.

I sipped my coffee and sat down at the kitchen table across from Izzie. "Is that good?" I asked, trying to make polite conversation with a three-year-old.

———

It was my first week on the job, and Jaxson was buried in his office.

I wasn't sure if he was ignoring me or giving me space and not preferential treatment.

Lucy hadn't so much as acknowledged my existence or the fact that Eagle Tactical now employed me. While she was at the front desk at the building entrance, I was shoved at the breakroom table with my laptop plugged into the nearest outlet.

It was clear they had made room for me to join them, and I'd take what I could get, office or not. I probably was lucky I even had a computer to work on; the keyboard was faded and worn.

The hallway was fine, it was a place to work.

I could almost see Jaxson if I leaned back in my desk chair, which I kept doing, the chair squeaking.

Lucy glanced over her shoulder at me, glaring with narrow eyes and a sharp jaw.

So maybe we weren't going to be friends like Emma and I had become.

I was okay with that, as long as she didn't bury me under paperwork.

A message popped up on the screen.

Mason, I need your help. Please track my phone and come for me. I wouldn't ask if this wasn't life or death— my death. Hazel

Who was Hazel, and why was I getting her message?

I still wasn't that friendly with Mason. We'd come to an understanding, or maybe it was the fact my cabin burned down that I had forgiven him.

It wasn't his fault for the fire, and the anger that I held toward him for selling me that crappy place seemed stupid now. Plus, he hadn't kept me from getting employed and helped Jaxson with the off-gridders who had threatened me.

We were almost friends. Well, not quite. He didn't hate me, and I didn't despise him, at least not anymore.

I stood, and the chair squeaked.

Lucy spun around in her seat, eyes wide. "Do you mind? Some of us are trying to get work done!" she snapped.

I didn't have a ton to do, granted it was my first week, and no one had assigned me any surveillance or backgrounds to research. I held my tongue.

I didn't need a new enemy. I had enough of them from my past.

My boots clunked over the tile floor, and I sauntered over to Mason's office. I knocked on the open door, not wanting to barge in unannounced.

"Yes, Ariella?" Mason glanced up from his computer. "What can I do for you?"

He didn't sound thrilled that I was bothering him, but I needed to make sure the message wasn't a joke, and it was real.

"I need you to see something that popped up on my computer," I said. I didn't want to elaborate. I wasn't sure who Hazel was to him, if anyone at all, and the doors were all open. The guys could all hear our conversation. I was trying to be discreet, for his sake.

His attention that had been on me briefly returned to his computer, his right hand clicking and scrolling with the mouse. "Declan can help you if you're having computer troubles."

"You need to see this," I said. When he didn't glance up or get up, I tried again. I guess I did need to spell it out for him. "Do you know someone by the name of Hazel? It sounds like she's in trouble."

He leaped out of the chair like it was on fire and followed me to my desk. He hunched forward, reading the message that remained on my screen.

"So?" I asked.

He studied the message for longer than necessary before he folded his arms across his chest. "Track her phone from the text. You can do that, can't you?"

Apparently, it was rhetorical. Before I could answer, he gave off orders.

"Send me her coordinates. If she's near Chicago, like I think she is, then I'll call one of my buddies with the U.S. Marshal's office, Colton. He'll lend us a hand."

"Will do." I sat back down at the desk and opened up a new window as I started a backend trace from the phone number where the text originated. Once I finished that, I was able to ping its location off the cell towers. Sure enough, Chicago.

I texted Mason the information from within our private network.

"Send her a text back. Let her know to go along with it."

I had no idea what Mason was talking about, but I relayed the message via text. I opened up a second window as I accessed the surveillance cameras along the highway. The vehicle they were in was headed for O'Hare International Airport.

"Where are you going?" I said to myself as I watched the screen.

Footsteps thumped inside Mason's office, and then the door slammed abruptly. Had I been that loud? I opened my mouth to apologize, but it didn't happen.

Mason was on the phone with someone. I could hear his muffled, gruff voice through the wall. He was talking to someone, perhaps this person Colton whom he had mentioned earlier.

How would the U.S. Marshals be able to help?

What had Hazel gotten herself into?

Hopefully, it wasn't a hoax, but the look that crossed Mason's face when he'd read the message on my laptop—it had to be authentic and she was in danger.

I wanted to do more. I couldn't let it go. I opened up the text message window for Hazel and sent another reply.

Can you tell me what's going on?

Maybe I could offer more help if we had more information. They were heading to the airport. If I knew what flight, perhaps I could hack into the ticketing system and put them on the no-fly list.

Mason?

I swallowed the lump in my throat.

Yes.

I texted back a little too quickly. Hopefully, he wouldn't be upset that I lied. She wouldn't ever have to know. And if I could help, why shouldn't I try?

What's my favorite color?

Shit. How was I supposed to know that? Was this a trick question? Radio silence. I didn't answer. She didn't respond. I screwed up.

Mason swung open the office door and stepped into the hallway. "Quit sending texts to Hazel. I can see everything on your monitor."

My stomach tanked.

Shit.

From where he stood, he couldn't see my computer screen. The only explanation was that he decided to hack my computer. When had he done that, after Hazel sent me the first message?

Mason threw on his coat and headed down the hall toward the front entrance. "Answer her. Tell her rainbow," Mason shouted to me over his shoulder.

Rainbow.

I breathed a sigh of relief. My fingers drummed against the desk. I waited for her to answer while I kept an eye on the monitor.

There were several surveillance cameras outside the airport. The black sedan she was in passed through the last one with no further exits. I linked into one of the satellite feeds, narrowed in on her coordinates. I needed to be with her, to see what was going on.

Where the hell had Mason gone? Didn't he want to watch?

I shifted uncomfortably in the seat, and Lucy glanced back over her shoulder at me, another death glare.

I grimaced but shrugged in response. I wasn't apologizing for my concern for Hazel or the squeakiness of the chair.

Two black SUVs swerved toward the sedan, forcing the vehicle to come to an abrupt halt.

I held my breath and watched as four men jumped out with guns draw and yanked open the back door.

The feed turned snowy and went dead.

CHAPTER THREE

Hazel

With my head bent down, I'd been quietly texting on my cell phone, when Franco spun around in his seat and yanked the phone from my grasp.

"Hey! Give that back!" From the backseat, I lurched forward.

Franco rolled down the window with the touch of a button and tossed my cell phone out onto the highway.

"You bastard!"

"You don't need a phone in Russia," Franco said. He rolled the window back up.

From the side mirror, I could see the smug look cross his face, pleased with his actions toward me.

I wasn't going to Russia, but time was running out.

We passed the last exit and drew closer to the airport's departures and arrivals. He didn't seem the kind of guy who would have us fly commercial, but it was a long flight.

If he forced me into the airport, I'd kick, fight, and threaten that I have a bomb, anything to keep me from going with him.

Why did he want me to go to Russia? Was that where he lived? Did my brother even care that Franco was taking me out of the country?

Two SUVs pulled up alongside us before one trapped the car at the front and the other around the back. The driver slammed on the brakes to keep from colliding with the SUVs. The sedan would have been no match.

Four men in street clothes, guns drawn, rushed at our vehicle.

One of them yanked the back door open—my saving grace.

"Hazel **Agron**, you're under arrest. You have the right to remain silent."

What the hell?

I thought they were helping me?

Go along with it. The words played over in my mind. Was this Mason's idea of a joke?

The man nearest to me dragged me out of the sedan and pushed me down onto the asphalt, face first. He held my hands behind my back, incapacitating me as he handcuffed me and read me my rights.

"Don't say anything!" Franco shouted at me.

Was he worried about himself or me? I doubted that he cared about what happened to me. He could buy a new bride. He'd find someone else to replace me, and I was fine with that.

The metal cuffs dug into my wrists as the man searched me for weapons before hoisting me to my feet. He escorted me to the back of his SUV and shoved me inside, handcuffs still on, my hands secured behind my back.

The man who had snapped on the cuffs was the first to speak. "Mason sent us." He shut the door and walked around to the opposite side before he climbed in beside me. "Sorry about the theatrics, but we had to make it look convincing."

"Can you get these off me?"

The SUV lurched forward, and he undid the cuffs. My wrists hurt from the metal. I rubbed the marks, hoping they'd vanish.

We circled the airport before heading for the highway. "I'm Colton Carr with the U.S. Marshals. We don't usually kidnap people from thugs."

"Maybe you should," I said and laughed softly. "Thanks for saving my life."

"Don't thank us yet. Those guys won't just go away. I've worked all my life to put guys like that behind bars," Colton said.

"Yeah." I glanced out the window as we pulled onto the interstate. What was the plan? Where would I go? "What happens now?"

I couldn't go home. Nikolai would hand me right back to Franco.

"We're taking you to a safe location."

"Like witness protection?" I asked. I could handle not talking to my brother ever again.

"We'll get papers for you and set you up with a new identity. Agent Stanford and Blakely will drive you across the country. It's too risky to put you on an airplane right now, and I spoke with Mason. We both agree it's best if you're far from Chicago."

———

I'd fallen asleep.

Big mistake.

The screech of tires woke me.

A strong and heavy scent of smoke filled the car, as I ducked in the backseat of the black SUV. I averted my stare.

Gunfire erupted from every side.

The driver, U.S. Marshal Stanford, who had been rather quiet for the past several hours, bled profusely from the chest, gasping and moaning, struggling to breathe.

I couldn't do much from the backseat.

The second agent, U.S. Marshal Blakely, who had been seated on the passenger side of the vehicle, was now slumped over from a bullet to the head.

The dark-haired driver gasped for breath. "Hold on," he shouted, his foot stomping on the gas as he steered us into the men with guns blazing, ramming into one of the black SUVs before backing up and doing it again.

My body jolted around in the SUV. My heart hammered in my chest.

The driver hit the vehicle's gas hard in reverse. I glanced over my shoulder out the broken back window as we catapulted past the men, the vehicles, and kept going away from the men who wanted me dead.

The pounding in my heart hadn't ceased. The moment of agony stretching onward.

I wanted to escape, to reach for the door and throw myself outside into the unknown and pray that I could outrun the bastards.

Nearly twenty hours ago, they'd wanted me in their possession like property, and Franco wanted to marry me.

Now bullets were spraying all around me. It seemed he changed his mind about the arranged marriage.

While I wanted to be brave, I was terrified. Shaking profusely in the back of the vehicle, I crawled onto the floor in a ball, sobbing as the SUV continued its course in reverse. U.S. Marshal Stanford no longer gasped for breath. He too was slumped over like U.S. Marshal Blakely, not offering me the least bit of protection.

I needed to get my shit together. I hadn't come this far, escaped the Russian mafia, only to wind up dead in the middle of nowhere.

My arm stretched out in an attempt to unfasten the U.S. Marshal's weapon. He no longer had any use for it. My fingers stretched, fiddling with the holster from my position on the floor, the vehicle still hauling backward toward who the hell knew what.

With a hard thud, the vehicle jolted and bounced, the suspension making me feel like we were on a springboard.

What the hell did they hit? I didn't dare glance up. The men and their gunshots sounded farther in the distance, faded and forgotten. Except they wouldn't have given up unless he'd injured them and forced them unable to follow when he hit the vehicles.

I couldn't quite remember how many impacts I had felt, at least three. Had there been four collisions? My body still jarred, my neck sore, and my stomach ached, but that had more to do with terror than anything else.

I carefully peered up, glancing out the back window.

Shit. We were heading toward a ravine.

"Stop! You have to stop the truck!" I didn't know why I screamed it at Stanford. He was dead. He couldn't help me. His foot remained like lead on the pedal, refusing to lighten up.

I couldn't tell how far the drop was, but the grass was gone, and there were mountains in the distance. It didn't look promising.

Forgoing the gun, I was out of time. I reached for the handle of the back door and popped it open.

The grass rushed by, the crisp winter air hit my cheeks. I had to do this if I wanted a chance at survival, and I did, more than anything.

I wanted a second chance at life.

I climbed with haste from the floor to position myself on the seat. I took two quick breaths before flinging myself out of the vehicle, hearing the crunch of metal down below.

I rolled as best I could out of the truck. My cheeks burned, my knees ached, and I had a terrible headache, but I was alive.

Gasping for breath, I lay staring up at the sky, grateful to still be alive.

After several seconds, I pulled myself from my reverie and stalked toward the ravine, staring down at the ledge where the vehicle had gone.

Down below, the SUV lay on its ceiling, crushed.

A part of me wanted to go down and make sure both U.S. Marshals were dead, but I already knew the answer. They'd died saving my life.

CHAPTER FOUR

MASON

It was the middle of the night. My phone buzzed, breaking me of sleep and comfort.

"What?" I wasn't a morning person, let alone a middle of the night wake my ass kind of guy.

"It's Colton. We've got a problem."

My stomach felt like it fell out. I ran a hand over my tired eyes and jumped out of bed. In the dark, I grabbed clothes and rushed into the bathroom.

"Shit." I flipped on the light, the brightness blinding. "What is it?" I wasn't ready for whatever he was about to spring on me.

Hazel was supposed to be on her way to Eagle Tactical for our protection. I had requested the best in Chicago, and that was Colton Carr.

"The U.S. Marshals were hit sometime in the past two hours. They didn't call in like they were supposed to, and their vehicle isn't moving. I've got GPS coordinates. I need you to go check it out."

"Why didn't you escort her?" I put my phone on speaker, yanked off my boxers, and threw them at the wall. He should have been in the vehicle. "I called you, Colton. I wasn't asking for the next best agents to help."

"Stanford and Blakely are two of the best the Marshals service has to offer. Do you want me to call the sheriff's office? You should know the mafia is involved, the Russian mob. They're going to keep trying to track her down."

I tugged on a clean pair of boxers and jeans, then threw on a sweater. I grabbed the phone and hurried with socks in my hand to fetch my shoes.

I didn't have a second to spare. Hazel's life was in danger. "I know that."

"Let me know what you find," Colton said.

"Yeah." I hung up the call with Colton, grabbed my car keys, and slipped on my socks and boots before I headed for my truck. "Fucking bastard," I muttered under my breath.

I asked him to do one thing, why couldn't he have listened?

The darkness of night enveloped the vast expanse of land, across the mountains and down the valley. The night sky was speckled with stars, a beautiful sight if I wasn't in a rush to find Hazel.

I slowed as I approached the coordinates and pulled over to the side of the road. I left the engine idle and the headlights on, unlocking the door.

I stepped out onto the street.

There was not another vehicle in sight for miles. Where the hell was the missing SUV? Had it been picked up already by a tow truck? That didn't seem right or likely on a Friday night. Especially if the vehicle had just recently been located.

I grabbed a flashlight from the truck and headed out into the field. Shining the light ahead of me, searching for any sign of Hazel seemed an impossible task.

She could have been anywhere by now.

She'd never been to Breckenridge. She wouldn't know how to find me.

My flashlight flickered, going out in the darkness.

"Damnit!" I threw the stupid flashlight into the distance but didn't hear the thud I expected.

Instead of a soft landing on the grass and field, there was a clank on metal in the distance.

I grabbed my phone from my pocket and used the flashlight feature to get a better look at the sound that I'd heard: a smashed-up vehicle in the ravine, crushed.

"Hazel!" I shouted and practically held my breath, listening for a response.

There were no noises from below. Darkness surrounded the vehicle.

I carefully catapulted down the side of the ravine, scaling the mountain. My boots slid under my feet, forcing me to lose my balance, but I caught myself before landing on my ass.

I'd made it to the bottom of the ditch. I glanced up the mountainside. It would be hell to climb back up but I could do it.

"Hazel?" I called out into the night.

No response.

I approached the smashed vehicle; bullet holes covered the body of the SUV. "What the hell happened?"

I crouched down, finding two male bodies. I checked them each for a pulse; neither were alive. There was no sign of Hazel.

That had to be good news. It meant she survived the crash, right?

Unless she'd been ejected out the windshield.

No, that was a horrible thought.

She had to be alive. Hazel was a fighter.

I dialed Aiden. He would know what to do. I didn't want to wake Jaxson. He had a kid at home, and

Lincoln had the restaurant. Declan would be useful in the office, so I patched Aiden and Declan in on a conference call.

"What's up?" Aiden asked. He didn't sound as tired as I felt.

"Aren't you just peachy?" Declan yawned. "What's going on?"

"I need help. It's regarding an off-the-books assignment." I didn't wait for them to answer. I headed back to my truck. Standing out in the field, searching for her wasn't doing a lick of good.

"You have my attention," Aiden said.

I hadn't wanted to involve them. I had hoped it could stay a private matter, but now it was extending into Eagle Tactical business. "A friend of mine is in trouble. She lives in Chicago, her father recently died, and it turns out her brother is head of the Russian mob."

"Shit. Drop it on us light, why don't you?" Aiden joked.

I ignored his attempt at humor. I wasn't laughing.

Hazel was out there, and men hunted her if they hadn't found her already. "I contacted Colton Carr yesterday afternoon when I received a message sent to our encrypted phone number. According to Colton, Hazel was sold as part of an arranged marriage set up by her brother." Bile rose in my throat just thinking about it. "Colton pulled her out of danger and put her en route to us when the U.S. Marshals were run off the road and attacked."

"Shit," Declan muttered. "Do you think whoever was after her picked her up? Is this a recovery mission?"

I ran a hand through my hair. "I hope not." I tugged on the strands before dropping my hand to my lap. "If we're lucky, she's still out there, hiding, waiting for our help."

"Tell me what you need," Declan said.

The phone connected to the car's Bluetooth.

I buckled myself and headed back onto the road.

Hazel wasn't just any girl; she was the first girl I loved. I still was in love with her, and everyone I had been with, I always compared to her.

"Aside from finding Hazel?" I gripped the steering wheel and did a U-turn, heading toward my house. "I'm going back to my house."

"Woke us up to tell us you were heading back to bed?" Declan snorted. "Gee, thanks."

"I've got night vision equipment and thermal detectors that I can use to find her. She's on foot, no more than two hours ahead of us. She would likely follow the road which would lead to town, but it means she has to navigate the mountain."

"We should be grateful it's not snowing. Hopefully, she has warm clothes and doesn't die of exposure," Aiden said.

Great.

Way to ruin my good mood. I hit the gas harder, needing to get home. If I were lucky, I'd find her first before the men who wanted her dead.

It worried me that the only abandoned vehicle had been the one she'd ridden inside. Lined with bullet holes, the other vehicle, or vehicles for that matter, were still out there. They hadn't been run off the road and down in the ravine. Which meant the men were at large, stalking Hazel like she was their prey.

"I'll rendezvous with you at your place," Aidan said. "Declan, head to the office. Maybe you can pull up something that'll help us figure out what the hell is going on."

If I found the men who were after Hazel first, I'd kill them with my bare hands.

CHAPTER FIVE

JAXSON

I'd found it difficult to sleep, tossing and turning through all hours of the night.

Usually, I was dead to the world when I slept, but the smell of Ariella's sweet scent mingled on my pillow and forced my mind to play over the night we shared.

Regret burned a hole in my stomach.

I drowned in her spicy aroma, and while the sheets didn't reek of sex, unfortunately, it still smelled blissfully of *her*. I buried my head beneath the thick blanket.

I hated that I hadn't told Ariella what she meant to me that night we shared, but now it felt a lifetime ago.

Funny how a few days could change your life.

My cell phone buzzed on the nightstand. I pushed the blanket down and grumbled.

I was not ready to be awake for work. My phone screen lit up the pitch-black bedroom.

With an exhausted gaze, I felt for the phone and hit answer. Shoving it against my ear, I shut my eyes, attempting to wake up, which seemed counterproductive.

"Eagle Tactical," I said. The call coming in wasn't one of the guys, and at this disgusting hour, it had to be a client. "This is Jaxson Monroe. Can I help you?"

"I certainly hope so," a deep gruff voice said. The man had a thick accent, Ukrainian or Russian. It was difficult to tell them apart. He cleared his throat. "I'd like to hire you to find my wife."

I sat up in bed and turned on the bedside lamp. "We don't typically handle domestic matters," I said.

I scooted to sit at the edge of the bed. My feet were planted firmly on the floor. The ground was cold, and the air outside of the warm blankets gave me goosebumps.

With the phone to my ear, I stood and headed straight for my dresser.

"This isn't a domestic matter. She was arrested yesterday morning. When I contacted the authorities to have her bond posted and released, she was never brought in for booking."

He had my attention. "Do you believe the authorities are involved in her disappearance?" That sounded a tad wild, even by my standards.

"No, that would be preposterous."

I opened the drawer to my dresser, grabbed a fresh set of clothes, and tossed the items to the bed. "It likely wasn't the authorities who picked up your wife."

"That is precisely my concern. I have many enemies. I would hate to think they came after my most prized possession. I can assure you that I will pay handsomely for her return to me."

While that was nice to know, it wasn't the only factor we considered. "Send me a photograph of your wife, along with her name and any distinguishing attributes—body piercings, scars, or tattoos, so that we can easily identify her."

I gave the gentleman my email address to send the information to me.

"I'd also like to meet you." It was a requirement. Anyone I hired as a client, I needed to know they were clean and not thwarting an active investigation.

"Of course. How does noon sound?"

I gave him Eagle Tactical's address and took his name and phone number before I hung up.

I showered and dressed in a hurry, shoved my phone into my back pocket, and shut off the lights to my bedroom.

Coming down the back stairwell directly to the kitchen, I put on a pot of coffee. I was going to need the extra jolt to stay awake today.

My body was sluggish, and I couldn't afford my mind to feel the same.

I stared at the coffeemaker, waiting for it to drip into the pot, the hiss of the water heating filling my foggy head.

"Who would kidnap a woman, pretend to be the authorities, and arrest her?" I said to myself. I leaned on the counter.

It didn't make sense. My gut instinct had me second-guess everything the man had said over the phone.

As soon as I received communication with him, I could track his phone, run a background check, and make sure he had nothing to hide.

It was what we did with all our clients that involved missing persons or abductions. In most cases, a spouse was involved or if it was a child, the parents. We didn't inform the parents or spouse that we looked into their financial, background, and past transgressions.

Soft footsteps pattered down the back stairwell. I straightened up and expelled a heavy breath. I could feel her presence, smell her sweet scent from across the room. Ariella had awoken.

"Did I wake you?" I hadn't intended the question to come out sharp and rough, but lack of sleep had done me in.

I wasn't a morning person without a solid six hours of sleep. I'd had far less, especially during training involving sleep deprivation and combat situations. This was neither of those, thankfully.

"No. I couldn't sleep. Is the coffee ready?" she asked.

I grabbed two mugs from the cabinet, flipping them over and placing them right side up. "Almost."

The coffee maker brewed and gurgled. Steam wafted from the back of the unit. It wasn't high tech or fancy, but it made a mean cup of coffee in a pretty decent amount of time. I hated to be kept waiting for my morning brew.

The last of the coffee dripped into the pot, and I poured two cups. I turned around and handed her a mug.

"Thank you," she whispered, staring at me.

I tried not to stare at her in the baggy flannel bottoms or the white t-shirt that clung to her breasts and revealed her nipples through her shirt. I failed miserably.

Her eyes widened, and she adjusted her shirt, one arm over her ample breasts, the other hand bringing the mug to her lips for her coffee.

I wanted to apologize; I knew I should have said something.

Instead, I glanced away, ran a hand through my morning hair, and pointed at the fridge. "Help yourself. I have to leave early this morning and get a head start on a new client."

"Oh. Anything I can help with?" Her eyes were full of promise and hope.

"No. There's no sense in you coming into work early. I'll run the background check this morning. When you get into the office, we'll see what we can have you work on."

She sipped her coffee, holding the mug to her lips as she took a long, slow gulp. "I don't mind coming in early."

"That's not a good idea." The two of us alone together, at the office, I had wild thoughts that involved bending her over my desk, lifting her skirt, and having my way with her.

Down, boy. I needed to cool it before she witnessed my arousal.

Her brow furrowed and her bottom lip jutted out. "Well, maybe it's not up to you." She put her coffee mug down hard and splashed remnants of what remained in her cup.

She got my attention. "Excuse me?" I stepped closer and stared down into those intense green eyes, an olive hue that sucked me in every time.

"I work for Eagle Tactical, not just you," she said. Her lips were firm and her jaw tight.

Desire made me want to lean down, wrap an arm around her waist and pull her tight against my skin.

I imagined lifting her jaw with my thumb, guiding her lips to mine. We were just inches apart.

Could she feel the heat radiate off my body and onto hers?

I ran a hand along the back of my neck and took a step back to recover from the fantasy. It couldn't happen. It shouldn't happen.

She was my employee, and while I had feelings for her, we'd made a commitment that we wouldn't act on those desires. I needed to respect that. I could use a cold shower.

"Did I do something to piss you off?" Ariella asked.

"Yes."

CHAPTER SIX

Hazel

The sky had grown dark, the distant sound of wild animals rustling through the grass. I kept in the meadow, the road just a few feet away, but I wouldn't walk on the paved surface.

Every time a car drove by, I stopped and ducked, lying against the grass, hiding from the men who were out searching for me, the same men who killed the U.S. Marshals.

Was it Franco or one of his goons? Either way, I wasn't safe.

My feet hurt and were blistered. I couldn't remove my shoes, though. That would be even more painful and stupid.

I hadn't anticipated that the U.S. Marshals would end up dead. This was all my fault.

I wrapped my arms around myself, the steep incline up the mountain difficult on my city girl calves.

I was not in shape, at least not for a hike of this magnitude. I was out of breath.

The higher I climbed, the more snow that covered the route.

The sound of tires on gravel and sludge forced me to freeze.

Someone was coming. Was it Franco?

I ducked down and held completely still, the forest surrounding me, allowing the vehicle to pass by as I went unnoticed by the driver.

The truck sped along the slushy snow and gravel road up the mountain. In the distance, through the forest, a porch light flickered.

I went off the road and through the brush, branches crunching under my feet.

I needed to take the shortcut. It was the only way to get out of the cold as fast as possible.

From my crouched position, I watched with fascination as a man stepped out from his truck and stood outside the building. It was too big to be a house.

It wasn't possible for him to see me. I took several more steps forward.

He couldn't know I was out here, right? My stomach flopped, and I wiped the sweat from my palms on my jeans.

He was nothing more than a silhouette, a handsome one at that from what I could tell, but it was dark, and within a few short moments, he had gone inside.

I hovered near the forest entrance and stepped into the slick, snowy muck. My shoes sunk into the dampness as I approached the building with a darkened sign that read 'Lumberjack Shack.'

Outside, two vehicles were parked. Was it the owner and a staff member? It didn't look open, but it was also very late or incredibly early, depending on how you looked at it.

I hurried toward the entrance and tried the door, curious if they kept it locked.

It didn't budge. I peered into the window; the chairs were situated upside down on the tables. The place was closed for the night.

Would they be opening soon? The sun might not come up for a few more hours, but if they served coffee and breakfast, then they would open.

The front door flung open, and I jumped, startled. It wasn't one of the men after me.

One glance at the gentleman, and he looked every bit a mountain man, with his thick beard and flannel shirt. "You almost gave me a heart attack!" I said.

"Me? You're the one peeking in through my windows." He studied me before glancing at the near-empty parking lot. "No car?"

There was no point in lying to him. "I walked." I wrapped my arms around myself, feeling tiny compared to his size and stance.

He could easily overpower me, but his eyes shone with mirth.

He didn't look scary, not like Franco.

"Come in, out of the cold," he said.

I didn't wait for him to ask twice or second guess himself. I followed on his heel and joined him inside. I exhaled a loud, long breath, the warmth of the building already soothing my aching and tender muscles.

The restaurant was dimly lit, and he fixed that right away, making my eyes hurt. I shielded my gaze until I adjusted to the brightness.

"You look like you could use a meal and maybe a shower," he said.

Yeah, I wasn't taking my clothes off. Fat chance of that, buddy. "Coffee sounds good." I needed caffeine to keep me awake.

I'd slept maybe an hour or two max in the car on the ride across the country. Had I known what would have gone down, I'd have tried sleeping more.

"I'm Lincoln," he said, introducing himself.

I stared at him, debating on whether I should give my name or lie. "Ashley Sinclair." The lie slipped out before I could even stop myself if I wanted to.

"It's nice to meet you, Ashley Sinclair." His eyes were tight, narrow as he headed behind the counter to put on a pot of coffee.

I followed, my feet leaving a mess of snow and ice on the inside of the restaurant floor. Lincoln would hate me. He'd hate me more when he realized I couldn't pay for the coffee. "Actually, I could just use a glass of water."

I didn't even have a dollar to my name. My wallet and possessions were back with Franco.

Everything I owned had been left behind.

"You look like you've been through a lot today. Coffee is on the house," Lincoln said.

"Really?" I couldn't believe he was nice just to be kind. People in Chicago weren't genuinely nice unless they wanted something and it was to their benefit.

"You remind me of someone," he said.

I climbed onto the stool to sit at the counter. "Well, I can assure you we've never met. I've never been to— where am I exactly?"

I'd been on my way to Mason at Eagle Tactical, but all I remembered was that it was somewhere in Montana.

"You really are in trouble if you don't know what town you're in," Lincoln said. He grabbed a mug and poured me a cup of coffee. "Cream and sugar?"

"Yes, please." He grabbed a handful of prepackaged creamers and sugar from under the counter.

"Thank you." I opened and dumped in two creamers before adding four packets of sugar.

"Holy cow, you have a sweet tooth." He laughed and ran a hand along his jaw. "Not sure I've ever seen someone use that much sugar in a single cup of coffee."

Had that been rude of me to do that without trying his coffee first? Wasn't all coffee the same, bitter and strong?

His cell phone buzzed, and he reached into his pants pocket. His brow furrowed as he answered a text message.

"Girlfriend?" I asked. He looked puzzled. Maybe she was mad that he wasn't in bed at this hour?

"No. Uh, my second job."

"Oh." I held the warm cup between both my hands, blowing on it softly before bringing the steaming mug to my lips. I inhaled the heat before letting my lips graze the porcelain. "So, you work here part-time?"

"I own the place," Lincoln said. He put his phone away, shoving it back into his pocket. "You said your name was Ashley?"

"Yeah, that's right." I took another swig of my coffee to keep myself preoccupied.

It was easier to lie when I didn't have to face the man who had whisked me out of the cold and warmed me up.

"Did you get separated from someone?" Lincoln asked. He poured himself a cup of coffee, black. "I can't fathom why you'd be out in the cold without a car."

"I live just down the road."

Lincoln smiled. "Of course. You probably come here all the time. I just have a terrible memory. A side effect of serving in the war."

I took another sip, my stomach grumbling from hunger.

"How do you like your eggs?" Lincoln asked.

"What's that?" Had he heard my obnoxious stomach growl too?

"I'm going to make you something to eat, and while I'd ordinarily offer pancakes, I'm betting you could use the extra protein. You look like you walked for miles outside. Am I right?"

Was it that obvious that I was in trouble? I covered my face with my hand. "I just got a little turned around coming from my house."

Another lie. How easily they slipped out.

"Right. How do you like those eggs? I'm going to make mine scrambled."

My mouth watered at the thought of food. It wasn't even being prepared yet, and already, my senses could imagine the taste. "That sounds delicious."

"I'll be right back," Lincoln said, heading to the kitchen.

I turned in my seat, keeping an eye on the door. I wanted to be alert and prepared in case the men who had run us off the road and shot at the SUV came back for me. I hadn't seen them since I had escaped out of the vehicle and jumped out before the SUV plunged down into the ravine. Did they presume I was dead?

Did Mason think I was dead?

As much as I'd stalked him online, I hadn't been able to find out if he was single or had ever married. There wasn't much about him outside of the obvious fact that he'd served in the army special forces and now was part owner of Eagle Tactical. It was almost like he wanted people to know that about him, and that was it.

I sipped the last of my coffee, desperate for another cup. I slid off the stool and came around behind the counter. Lincoln was busy in the kitchen. Hopefully, he wouldn't mind me intruding for a second cup.

The bell on the door rang as someone opened the door and headed inside.

I ducked behind the counter and snapped my mouth shut.

"Hello?" a thick Russian accent reverberated through the restaurant. His voice boomed and echoed with each heavy step he took.

Fuck!

A second set of steps separate from the man who spoke approached the counter.

"Can we get some service?" another Russian said.

He smacked the top of the counter and lifted the cup that I'd just poured.

CHAPTER SEVEN

MASON

I pulled up in the parking lot after hearing back from Lincoln that a strange girl had shown up at the restaurant.

It had to be Hazel.

Who else would have wandered there on foot in the middle of the night? His text had been brief but detailed enough to indicate the girl was in trouble.

I needed to catch him up to speed, but that would wait. I parked next to an unfamiliar SUV and stepped out of my truck.

Bullet holes lined the outside body of the SUV. I grabbed my gun and hurried around to the back of the restaurant, through the door that had been left unlocked for deliveries.

The sun hadn't risen yet, but the delivery trucks usually came before the restaurant opened with customers.

I tore inside, gun drawn, through the kitchen, meeting Lincoln.

"Where is she?"

"Can we get some service?" a thick Russian accent echoed from the other side of the door.

"Out there," Lincoln said. He reached beneath the kitchen counter and grabbed his spare gun. "I left her for five minutes to make breakfast, I swear—"

I held up a hand for him to be quiet. They mustn't have seen her, or they'd have taken her and left already.

I grabbed a serving tray and used it to hide my gun. Lincoln followed directly behind me so they wouldn't see his weapon, either.

"Can I help you gentleman?" I asked, stepping out from the kitchen.

I tried to ignore the bright auburn hair nestled in the crook of the counter, hidden out of sight. She trembled on the floor, her body tight like a peanut, like in one of those drills we learned back in elementary school.

"Kitchen isn't open yet. We can get you coffee to go."

The men exchanged wayward glances. "What kind of restaurant isn't open for breakfast?"

"The kind that doesn't serve—breakfast," Lincoln said between gritted teeth.

His hands were clenched at his sides as he came around my side to block the entrance to the kitchen and behind the counter where Hazel had stashed herself.

Had she seen the men coming? How had she known to hide?

"Know where I might find a bed?" the man with thinning black hair asked. His muscles protruded from his shirt.

Why the hell wasn't he wearing a coat? What idiot ran around in winter without a jacket?

"There's no vacancy this side of the mountain," I said. I didn't want either man staying in town.

"Right." They exchanged a quick, cursory glance before lifting their weapons.

Guns drawn toward us, bullets flew through the air.

I ducked by the counter and scooted behind it with Hazel. Her eyes met mine.

I gestured for her to stay down.

Lincoln fired off a round of shots, and I stood from behind the counter, doing the same, landing several blows to their chests and then a final kill shot to the heads.

"Shit," Lincoln muttered, coming around to kick the guns away from their hands.

He felt their pulses, a habit of never being too careful, just to make sure they were as dead as they looked. "Do you think insurance covers the damage?"

I laughed under my breath. That was his biggest concern?

I helped Hazel stand. She trembled in my arms, her eyes wide, full of terror. "It's okay. You're safe now," I said. "They can't hurt you."

"I'm not worried about them," Hazel whispered. "It's Franco I'm afraid of."

"Get her out of here," Lincoln said. "Take her to Eagle Tactical. I'll clean up this mess and phone the local sheriff."

"He's going to want all of our statements." While I wanted to protect Hazel, I wasn't going to break the law for her, either.

We had killed two men in self-defense, but she was a witness and the reason the men had been in the restaurant. We couldn't leave her out of the story.

Besides, the sheriff and I had a good relationship. We consulted for the local police department from time to time and helped them when they needed assistance.

It would be wise to let them know what they were in for. It was possible that this wasn't anywhere close to being over.

"Yes, I know." Lincoln shooed us out of the restaurant. "I'll tell him to come by your office. Just get her out of here and keep her out of danger."

I glanced out the window, making sure there weren't any other vehicles or men loitering outside before I opened the door and led her out to my truck.

"Thanks for saving my life," Hazel said.

I tried not to stare at her, but damn, it was hard. I hadn't seen her in over a decade.

I grinned like a damned idiot and opened the truck door. "Hop in."

Gosh, it was good to see her again. Though I'd have preferred it to be under different circumstances.

I offered her a hand as she struggled with making it up on the running board. Once inside the truck, I shut the door and hurried around to the driver's side.

I climbed in, pulled out of the lot, and kept my attention on the road. I made sure that no one followed us.

"How have you been? Well, I mean minus all this," I said.

What a stupid question. Since when did I become a bumbling fool around the ladies?

Hazel had captured my interest and my heart in high school. We'd gone to boarding school together in Chicago. While my parents had lived in Montana, I'd gotten into a mountain of trouble, and they'd sent me to live with my grandma in Chicago.

That hadn't lasted.

Two weeks with her, and I had the option of attending military school or boarding school.

Hazel sighed long and loud. Her stare was on me the entire time.

"Do I have something on my face?" I asked. I rubbed at my forehead.

"No. It's just, I haven't seen you in so long. I want to hug you and then hit you for breaking my heart," Hazel said.

What? When had I broken her heart?

I tried mulling it over, but my attention was quickly diverted when a black town car headed north up the road.

On instinct, I reached out and guided her head down so that as the vehicle passed up, they wouldn't see her face.

"More Russians?" Hazel's voice trembled.

They didn't look like the goons from earlier, but it was still peculiar to see anyone who wasn't a local at this hour.

I waited until the vehicle passed to answer. "I don't think they were with the guys back there at the restaurant."

There were guests who stayed at the resort and came up to the restaurant or hiked on the local trails, but that didn't happen until daylight.

Something felt amiss, but I didn't want to worry her.

The sun was almost about to peek from the horizon. I stomped on the gas.

It would be easier to move in the dark.

Daylight would make Hazel stand out with that fiery auburn hair. I'd have to send Ariella to the store to pick up hair dye and probably a few other necessities.

One thing at a time. The first, was making sure she survived.

I pulled up out front of Eagle Tactical and rushed her inside the building, securing the deadbolt the moment we were inside. "Come with me."

I led her down the hallway and to my office. I didn't want her anywhere near the entrance, and while there was a back door, it wasn't easily accessible with the snow and ice along the path leading up to it. No one ever shoveled the back walk.

She followed me into my office, her footsteps soft and invisible against the tile while my strides were loud and forceful as I announced my presence.

Aiden and Declan poked their heads out of their respective offices. "Good morning," they said in unison.

"This is Hazel. Hazel, meet Aiden and Declan," I said, introducing them.

"Glad you made it in time to the restaurant," Declan said. "Lincoln texted us the firefight was over, or we'd have sprinted over to help."

"We had it handled." We weren't outmatched or outgunned. I'd been through worse, countless times. "I'm going to take Hazel into my office, chat with her in private for a few minutes. The sheriff will come by in a bit for our statements. Let him in, would you? Also, keep the door locked. We can't be too careful."

I didn't wait for their answer. I shut the office door almost in their faces. They took a knowing step back; I was in charge since this was my case.

Hazel was a priority, *my* priority.

"Have a seat," I said, offering her the sofa in the corner. I approached the storage cabinet and fumbled through a few trinkets before landing on one that would have to do.

"What are you looking for?" she asked.

I showed her the golden bangle, sliding it on past her hand, letting it dangle on her wrist.

"I'm more of a silver kind of girl," Hazel said.

"Keep that on until everything is resolved with Franco. Okay?" We didn't have much in terms of tracking devices upstairs.

The basement housed our surveillance equipment, specialty gadgets, and a high-end server with a faraday cage to keep hackers out while we were able to infiltrate even the toughest security. We also had weapons locked away, but we'd made an agreement early on that only those of us who worked for Eagle Tactical would be the only ones to know about the basement or what was down there.

I wasn't ready to leave Hazel unattended, even to go downstairs and search for a different style of tracking device. The bangle would suffice, and it looked good on her.

She stared at the bracelet on her wrist. A faint smile played at the corner of her lips. "If I'd have known you were going to give me jewelry, I'd have visited you a lot sooner."

I turned the desk chair around and slunk into the leather, facing her. "It's a tracking device. As long as you're wearing it, you'll be safe."

"Isn't it rather obvious?" She thrust her arm at me, the bracelet swinging on her wrist. "It's not very discreet."

We had discreet high-tech trackers, but the fact was I wasn't letting her out of my sight. It was a formality, just in case something happened.

"It doesn't have to be. I'm not letting Franco anywhere near you." I sat across from her, clasping my hands together in my lap. "I want to know everything about the bastard. Lay it on me, all of it."

Her fingers played with the bracelet as she spoke. "I don't know much about him. My brother, the new head of the Russian mafia, sold me to his second in command."

"He sold you?" My fists clenched, and I stood, disgusted with any man who thought a woman was his property. I couldn't sit still; my legs wouldn't allow it. I paced the length of my office, practically wearing a hole in the tile. "Keep going."

I needed more details.

As much as it sickened me to hear it, I wanted to know *everything*.

"Nikolai thought it was high time I married and arranged the purchase to Franco Ivanov."

I stopped pacing when I recognized the withdrawn and hesitant look cross her face.

I bent down, clasping her one hand in mine, and with my other hand, I brought my fingers into her bright red tresses, guiding her chin to meet my stare.

"I will not let anything happen to you. I promise you, Hazel, you're safe with me."

"I'll never be safe again," she rasped. "Franco won't stop looking for me."

Her hands trembled, and she pulled away to wipe the salty tears that glistened at the corners of her eyes.

"I mean, maybe he will, but if that's the case, it's only because he wants me dead. They killed two U.S. Marshals, Mason. Men like that don't stop. They'll never give up searching for me. I wouldn't be surprised if Franco demands his men return me—dead or alive."

I wouldn't let that happen to Hazel. She meant too much to me, and besides, it was my job to protect those who couldn't protect themselves. "First, you're going to have to speak with the sheriff. When you're done, I'm going to have you relocated and a protective detail with you at all times."

"I thought I was staying here." Hazel patted the sofa. "I can sleep here. It's really no big deal."

Was she ridiculous? While we had decent security at Eagle Tactical, it was a prime location for Franco to search for her.

We couldn't house her with one of our Eagle Tactical members, which was against protocol, and she had indirectly hired me when she reached out requesting help.

Besides, I couldn't watch her twenty-four-seven. It would be better, for her sake, to have the entire team helping her.

Jaxson swung the door open, oblivious to what was happening. He hadn't been kept in the loop, and that was my fault.

His brow furrowed, pointing at Hazel.

"We have a new client," Jaxson said. "He called this morning and hired us for our services to find his missing wife. I'm sorry. We haven't met. I'm Jaxson Monroe."

"Ashley Sinclair," Hazel said with a forced grin as she held out her hand.

CHAPTER EIGHT

JAXSON

"How nice to meet you, Ms. Sinclair," I said and stepped closer, offering out my hand.

One glance at her, and without a doubt, I recognized her from the picture on my phone as Hazel Agron.

What was Mason doing with her? "Can I have a word with you, alone?" I asked Mason.

"Sure. I'll just be a sec," he said to the woman seated on the sofa in his office.

I stepped out into the hallway and gestured for him to come into my office.

I forced the door closed harder than intended. It slammed.

"Something on your mind?" Mason asked. It was just the two of us.

"That girl you think you're protecting, she's not who she says she is."

Why was Hazel in his office lying about her identity? Did Mason realize that he'd been deceived?

I wanted to be reasonable. I was still running background on Nikolai as well as Hazel. The information had been squeaky clean for both of them. Not so much as a parking ticket.

Mason's eyes shined and the corners of his lips curved upward. "I know that, but how do you know that?" he asked.

I slumped into my plush office chair and slid it around to face Mason. "Have a seat." I gestured to the empty seat in my office.

He exhaled loudly through his nose and sat down. "What's going on, Jaxson?"

"I received a call early this morning from a new client requesting our help in locating his missing wife."

"Missing wife? Tell me you didn't hire him." Mason leaned forward on his knees, his head in his hands. "Did you miss what happened with your girlfriend yesterday morning?"

My jaw clenched and my hands bunched at my side into fists. "She's not my girlfriend, and no, I was busy running background checks for Blue Sky Resort, again. I'm surprised they hired us after the last time, with Ariella."

Hunched forward, his elbows on his knees, he ran a hand through his short, cropped hair. "Please tell me we didn't take the Russian mob on as a client," Mason said.

What the hell was he talking about? "She's with the Russian mafia?"

I'd done preliminary searches, and everything had come back squeaky clean.

My specialty was in the field. I wasn't a hacker. I didn't know how to access what wasn't easily accessible. Declan was the go-to guy for that, and

Ariella, I had a feeling she could probably keep up with him, with her former C.I.A. training.

I shouldn't have turned Ariella's offer down earlier that morning. I'd been foolish and self-indulgent.

"She's not willingly with the Russian mafia," Mason said and cleared his throat. "Hazel's brother is the head of the mob in Chicago. I'm guessing you already know that's her real name."

We didn't keep secrets from one another. "Why didn't you tell me you accepted her call for help?"

I didn't like the position that this put our team in; hiring both sides wasn't advisable. We weren't mediators, and this was the mafia we were dealing with, not a messy divorce.

"Aiden and Declan already know," Mason said. He held out his hands, palms upward. "Lincoln knows too."

"Lincoln?" I stood, the chair squeaking as it slid behind me. "Why am I the last to know?"

"Because you have your head so far up your ass, Monroe. You buried yourself in your office to avoid the hottie out there," Mason said, pointing at the door. "If you spent five minutes not being narcissistic, then you would have seen what's right under your nose."

It was a good thing Mason wasn't my employee and we were equals or I'd have fired his ass and thrown him out the front door.

"You're out of line, Reid." If he was going to call me by my last name, two could play at that game.

A soft knock rapped at the door. "What?" I shouted and yanked the office door open.

Ariella stood on the other side, her eyes wide as she averted her stare from me to Mason.

"Don't shoot the messenger," she said, "but the sheriff is here for your statement, Mason."

"Your statement? What the hell, Mason?" How much had I missed?

Mason stood and brushed past me without another word. He led Sheriff Nelson into his office and shut the door behind himself.

"What the hell is going on?" I asked.

Declan and Aiden had disappeared down the hall, and Ariella slunk into the seat at her desk, attempting to look small and invisible.

"Ariella?" I wanted someone to tell me what the hell I'd missed. It seemed she knew about Hazel. What else did she know?

"Yes?" her voice squeaked as she met my stare.

"My office, now." I stomped into my office and didn't turn around.

I could hear her soft footsteps as they fell against the floor.

She left the office door open and probably hoped Declan or Aiden might save her ass.

"What can I do for you?" Ariella asked. She stood with her arms tight against her side, her shoulders slumped.

"Have a seat."

"Are you firing me?"

"What?" I laughed under my breath at the absurdity of her question. "Do I have a reason to fire you?"

Had she done something that I wasn't aware of yet?

She didn't move from her position on the floor just a few feet away. Her body was practically a statue, except for the slight tremble.

"I don't believe so," she stammered.

"Good." I pinched the bridge of my nose. Five seconds, and she was giving me a headache. Maybe I was blaming her for something that wasn't her fault. She didn't know the mess I'd gotten Eagle Tactical involved in by accepting Franco as a client. Shit. Franco. He planned on coming to the office around noon. "I need your help."

She nodded but didn't say a word.

"The minute the sheriff is done with his interview, I need you to take Hazel to the resort."

"Blue Sky Resort?" Ariella asked. Dread crossed her face. She looked like she might be sick.

"You can do that, can't you? I need you to rent a room. No one will think anything of it since no one knows you work for us." It would be an easy solution for the time being. I needed to get Hazel out of the office and some place safe.

"I—yeah, I can do that." She rolled her lips tight between her teeth.

I didn't imagine it would be easy for her to step foot back in the resort that had fired her and where she'd been assaulted. The job itself wasn't easy.

"I don't think Mason is going to want to leave her side," Ariella said. "They have some type of past connection, history together."

"They do?" She knew more about Hazel than I did. "What else do you know?"

She appeared to relax under my scrutiny. Ariella took another step and came to sit down in the chair that Mason had vacated a few minutes prior. "Hazel reached out to him for help," Ariella said. "Maybe I should start from the beginning."

"That would be good." I perched myself at the edge of the wooden desk and listened to her recant how she'd received a message on her laptop and that Mason had been involved in contacting the U.S. Marshal's office, someone by the name of Colton, to help extract her.

I knew Colton. We'd served in the military together.

"Stay here," I said and headed out into the hallway and to Aiden's office for the safe stashed in the wall, hidden away in the closet.

Aiden and Declan went silent the minute I stepped into their office. "Don't mind me," I said and went right for the safe.

"Something we can help you with?" Declan asked.

"Yes. I need to get Ariella a credit card to get a room and check-in early at the resort," I said.

I opened the safe and flipped through the materials that were available.

"And you don't think whoever runs the check-in desk will notice she's using a fake name?" Declan grinned. "Are you trying to set her up to get arrested?"

Shit. "No." The hotel would require a credit card for incidentals when checking in. "I'll book the room online and have her check-in and use her own card."

Aiden shook his head. "You're getting sloppy."

It was the lack of sleep. I didn't do my best work after being up all night. "I didn't sleep well last night."

Declan and Aiden exchanged a glance.

"What?" I growled at the two of them.

"Your sexual frustration is killing all of us. Please, go home. Shower, sleep, bluff the squirrel," Declan said.

I choked out a laugh, embarrassed.

I couldn't believe what they suggested. My glance shot out toward the open door and Ariella, who had stepped out into the hallway.

Fuck me.

I'd pretend she didn't hear what Declan said because I wished I hadn't heard it.

Her footsteps grew louder as she knocked on the open door.

"I thought I told you to stay in my office?" I threw my arms up into the air. "Why does no one listen to me around here?" I stomped past Ariella on the way out of Declan's office.

Ariella didn't move.

"Are you coming?" I shouted over my shoulder.

"Do I have to?" I heard her mutter under her breath. My cell phone buzzed in my pocket. I grunted and held up a finger to tell her to hold on a second while I checked the caller ID. It was Skylar.

It was like she knew when I was busy and had to call and pester me.

What now? I couldn't deal with her. I rejected her call and took a long, slow breath to regroup.

I turned around to yell at Ariella to hurry up when I discovered she had already followed, silent and practically invisible on my heel.

I stopped abruptly when I turned around to face her, and she nearly slammed into my chest. Her reflexes were fast and she caught herself before we collided.

I almost wished she had knocked into me. It would have given me an excuse to touch her.

"I'm going to pay for your room in advance over the internet. If anyone asks, including Emma, tell her that you're staying at the resort until insurance is figured out with your house," I said.

She needed to be prepared for questions, especially returning to Blue Sky Resort.

"I've got it handled. Don't worry," she said, giving me a reassuring smile. She reached out and rested a hand on my arm. "Are you okay?" Her voice was soft and sweet, like honey.

I wanted to pull her against me, touch her, taste her, and let the agony that filled my heart disappear.

"Just tired," I said. Her touch was soft yet firm. I pulled away. We couldn't do that or be that for each other.

She shuffled her feet. It was the most I'd seen her move all morning. "I didn't hear Izzie last night. Did she keep you up? I must have slept through it."

"It wasn't Izzie."

I didn't elaborate.

How could I?

The smell of her scent on my pillow kept me awake all night.

She'd think I was crazy if I told her the truth. Maybe I was going slowly insane, needing my next fix of *her*.

I hadn't ever felt the desire as strong as I did now, a deep ache that tore away at me every second that I couldn't touch her or be with her.

We'd only shared one night together.

It had been wonderful, but I had to push it out of my head. Exhaustion had crept over me and made me desperate.

CHAPTER NINE

ARIELLA

Why hadn't Jaxson been able to sleep? If it wasn't Izzie, what had kept him up all night?

I'd slept great. The guest room hadn't been as cozy as the first night that I had curled up under his sheets and he'd held me, but neither of us spoke about that incident. He'd been there to look after me, that was all.

"I promise I'll be out of your house soon," I said.

"Good," he said, his tone gruff. He rubbed at his jaw, not able to meet my stare.

"Did I do something to piss you off? Because if I remember correctly, I should be mad at you. Not the other way around."

That caught his attention. His gaze fell down to my eyes and then my lips.

Had the heat come on? The room was several degrees warmer than it had been just a few minutes earlier.

Jaxson didn't answer me. He didn't say a word. He didn't have to. His brow furrowed, and his eyes looked tired.

"I shouldn't have said anything," I muttered under my breath. I'd probably just gone and made things a lot worse for the two of us.

"No," he said, his voice hoarse. He grabbed my arm and pulled me closer, invading my personal space.

I struggled not to meet his stern gaze that studied me.

What was he thinking? My breathing came out in soft, shallow breaths.

His proximity was all it took to further heighten my senses.

A simple touch of his hand sent a spark of lightning through my body, warming me, creating an ache of need that I'd squashed down to nothingness.

"I want you to talk to me, Freckles."

Hearing him use the nickname he'd given me was my undoing.

I couldn't stand there in front of him and pretend that everything would be all right. It wasn't fine.

My heart ached beyond measure. He'd left in the middle of the night after our first intimate night together.

There'd been no note, no discussion later of it.

"Was I just a girl you wanted to get into bed?" I hadn't intended the question to come out quite so harshly.

Jaxson took a step back like I'd slapped him. His eyes widened, and he ran a hand through his hair. "Come with me," he commanded.

"Are you always this grumpy?" I snipped, irritated that every second I spent time with him, he'd grown to be a different person. Was this what he was like at work? How did the guys stand it?

He quirked an eyebrow, not looking the least bit amused by my question. "I'm not the grumpy one," he retorted.

He grabbed my hand, tugged me into his office, and shut the door abruptly at my heels, his hands letting go of mine.

I tried not to jump when he'd startled me, but I wasn't great at hiding my emotions or reactions, apparently. "What are you doing?" I didn't feel in danger or threatened, but Jaxson also hadn't been himself, at least what I knew of him.

"We need to talk." He gestured for me to come closer while he perched himself at the edge of his desk.

I stood, arms folded, staring at him. I wouldn't sit down. "Whatever you need to say, say it."

I was tired of his antics. Jaxson had been warm, protective, and kind when I'd gotten to know him, but every minute that I was in his presence, it seemed like I could do nothing right. It had only been a few days at work, and maybe I needed to give us time to figure it out.

He exhaled a heavy sigh and folded his arms across his chest, mirroring my position. "I think it would be best if you stayed with Hazel at the resort. I'll make sure when I book the reservation that I request a room with two queen beds."

"Excuse me?" I didn't back down, challenging him. "You brought me in here, shut the door, to tell me to what, get out of your house?"

Was he not man enough to do it in front of his buddies?

"No. That's not—" he groaned when his phone buzzed.

Skylar's name popped up on the screen. "Fuck." He rejected her call.

It seemed he wasn't only avoiding me. Had his change in mood been a result of Skylar coming to visit? "You should take that call; it might be important," I said.

"It's not," Jaxson said.

I stared at him, surprised he hadn't taken the opportunity as an excuse to end the awkwardness between us.

"You think I'm a jerk for not answering Skylar."

That wasn't what crossed my mind. "No. You're a jerk for not saying goodbye, texting me, or leaving a note after we slept together. You're a grumpy bosshole at the office and lately at home. If I had realized how much my presence irritated you, I wouldn't have accepted the job."

I didn't wait for his response. I jetted out of his office in time as the local sheriff was on his way out the main door.

"Hi, Hazel, I'm Ariella," I said, offering her my hand as I introduced myself to her. "I'm going to take you someplace safe."

Hazel glanced from me to Mason. He gave her a warm smile and a nod. "I'll be right behind you in my truck. We just need to make sure that no one knows we're together."

———

I hadn't been back to the Blue Sky Resort since the attack.

I still needed to pick up my paycheck for the time that I'd worked there but hadn't wanted to step foot in that place again.

I pulled into the parking lot.

The building loomed over us.

Mason was just a few minutes behind. He didn't intend on coming in the main entrance. He'd let himself in via the back and then take the elevator up to our floor.

Hazel didn't have anything with her. No bags. No clothes. She wore Mason's sweatshirt and a baggy pair of sweats, the hood over her head.

She kept her face down, her hands shoved into her pockets, and tried to appear inconspicuous.

I could do this. It was an easy assignment. All I had to do was check into the hotel lobby, get the key card and take Hazel up to the room, which would be our room.

I hadn't broken the news to her that I'd be rooming with her indefinitely.

"Everything okay? Are you going to be sick?" Hazel asked.

Emma stood behind the registration desk. We were friends, and while I was glad to see her, I hadn't spoken with her since before I'd been fired. She hadn't known about the assault and abduction.

Had she known why I'd been fired, that I had another name, or that I'd previously been employed by the C.I.A.?

"Ariella," Emma said, a dutiful smile on her face. It was the same gleeful expression that she gave all the guests at the resort.

Hazel glanced from Emma to me. I could tell she had questions, but thankfully she didn't start asking them.

"I have a reservation," I said, digging out my wallet from my purse.

"Under which name?" Emma asked. The smile disappeared from her sunny disposition.

She knew. "Ariella Cole." It was my legal name and maiden name. I'd changed it after the divorce. I was formerly Ariella Ryan, the wife of Benjamin Ryan. He'd been convicted of several felonies for embezzlement, money laundering, the list went on. And now she knew.

Emma stood behind her desk. Her fingers tapped away at the keyboard as she stared at the screen.

Did she see the reservation? Was she just trying to take her time and fluster me? I thought we were friends, but the cold shoulder she gave me was my answer.

"Do you have a credit card, Ms. Cole?" Emma asked. "I will need one with the name Ariella Cole on it."

I handed over my credit card. "Of course. Do you need to see my government-issued identification too?" I flashed my driver's license at her, and I was ready to pull it out of my wallet from behind the plastic screen if she wanted to see it.

She tapped away at the keyboard. "No need." Another minute, and she retrieved two room keys, running them through the scanner as she assigned us a hotel room. "I've got two queen beds on the third floor. Can I help you with anything else?"

She handed us the keycards and wrote down our room number.

"I'm sure you can find your way to the elevator."

"Thank you," I forced out, snatched the keycards, and stalked away from the registration desk with Hazel at my side.

"Wow. Did you steal her boyfriend?" Hazel joked.

I pushed the elevator button to go up. "Something like that." I hadn't even considered that she might have been pissed about Jaxson.

Hazel didn't need to know about my past. My job was to look after her and get her to the hotel room.

Mason would be joining us anytime now.

We stepped into the elevator, just the two of us. I pushed the button to the third floor and hit the 'close doors' button repeatedly as a gentleman rushed toward the elevator.

I didn't want to be trapped with him, just in case he was after Hazel.

The doors slammed shut and the elevator ascended up to the third floor. I breathed a sigh of relief. I was probably making something out of nothing. He was probably just a guest at the resort.

Hazel remained quiet, and I stepped out of the elevator first when the doors opened. Mason was already in the hallway and stood outside our assigned room.

They worked at lightning speed. Declan must have provided him with the room number by hacking into the resort's system.

I opened the door with the room key, and Mason went in first, flipped on the light, and checked the bathroom and closet.

"Are you sure it's safe?" she asked, glancing around the room with a frightful gaze as she followed Mason in.

I shut the door behind myself and locked it, using the deadbolt.

"Yes. Keep the curtains shut. Someone will be with you at all times." Mason sat in a chair in the corner of the room that faced the door, his back to the wall.

"I'll be staying the night," I blurted out. "Jaxson uninvited me to stay with him."

I was pretty much homeless. With no insurance on my house and the fire that had destroyed the property, I had nothing.

"Wow," Mason said. He ran a hand through his short, cropped hair. "You do know why he's been an ass lately, don't you?"

I didn't answer his question. I wasn't sure. I assumed it had to do with me and he regretted that Eagle Tactical had hired me.

"Jaxson's sexually frustrated. I see the way he looks at you," Mason said.

"Like he wants to kill me?" I laughed.

"The man needs to get laid. He stares at you like you're the prize he wants at the fair."

It was absurd. "That can't be it." I didn't want to believe that he'd treated me like crap and kicked me out of his house because he wanted to have sex with me. "Oh my gosh! I'm an idiot. Jaxson's probably upset that he can't bring another woman over with me living in one bedroom and his sister in another."

"I'm pretty sure he doesn't want anyone else," Mason said, spelling it out for me.

Was that true? "I don't know, Mason. You didn't see him this morning in the office or when we're at his house. He can barely look at me."

"I'd have the same problem if I was living under the same roof as the woman I love and can't have," Mason said.

His gaze moved from me and locked on Hazel.

I could feel the sexual tension brewing between them with just a simple look. I cleared my throat and backed up toward the door.

"I need to head to the store and pick up a few things for Hazel. She's going to need clothes, toiletries, anything else?" I asked.

"Get her hair dye and sheering scissors," Mason said. "We can't take a chance that she'll be easily spotted by Franco or his buddies. Ariella, I want you to know you're welcome to stay in the extra bed. One of us will be here keeping watch over Hazel, protecting her, but you don't have to go back to Jaxson's if you don't feel comfortable."

"Thanks."

I wasn't sure what I was going to do, but having the option to stay at the hotel eased my mind more than I thought it would. I'd need to pick up my clothes, the few belongings I'd purchased after moving in with Jaxson.

"Do you need anything else?" I asked Hazel.

"Chocolate and maybe a box of condoms." She grinned, casting a glance at Mason.

Mason groaned. "Woman, you are going to make my job difficult. I can see it now."

"You haven't seen anything yet." Hazel winked at Mason.

I took that as my hint to leave.

CHAPTER TEN

Hazel

"She seemed nice," I said the minute the hotel room door closed.

Mason secured the lock before sitting back down on the chair.

"Ariella? Yeah, we haven't worked together long," Mason said. He didn't elaborate.

Okay. So maybe talking about Ariella wasn't the best conversation starter.

I turned off the television. It had been years since we'd seen one another. I didn't want to watch T.V. or pretend like what we were doing was normal.

I wanted to catch up with Mason, discover every flaw, and see how much he'd changed since high school when we were practically kids and inseparable.

"I've missed you," I said and stood from the bed. I toed off my shoes and sauntered across the room toward Mason.

"Hard to tell since you never called." His voice was gruff, his expression hard. There was so much he didn't know, and I didn't know how to tell him.

"Neither did you," I said.

We were both at fault for letting our lives go separate ways.

He'd gone into the army, and I was supposed to attend college in California. I had promised to write to him and he had every right to be angry. I'd broken that promise.

"I'd ask how you've been, but I can see that's not a story with a happy ending," Mason said.

"It could be," I said. I towered above him and straddled his legs before sitting down on his lap, facing him.

I wanted to jump back in time, have him take me with him, far from Chicago. It was too late to change the past, but I wanted to forget the time spent apart.

"Tell me you don't have a girlfriend or are married." I reached for his left hand, bringing his digits up to my face.

My lips latched onto his empty ring finger, grateful he appeared to be single.

"Hazel," his tone warned me to stop.

I didn't listen. I never listen.

I rolled my hips, teasing him, practically giving him a lap dance. With my fingers in his hair, I leaned forward, pushing my breasts against his chest.

I wanted him more than I wanted anyone in my life. I'd loved him since we were fourteen. He was the one who had gotten away.

"Promise you'll protect me."

I needed him like I needed air to breathe. He had no idea what I'd done to survive.

His forehead rested against mine. His warm, strong palm rested at my lower back. "You have my word. I won't let anything happen to you," Mason said.

I tangled my fingers in his hair.

His eyes shut.

My breath caressed against his lips. I wanted to kiss him. I needed to feel alive as I craved that connection with him.

He was my chance at freedom from Franco, at the prospect of a normal life, not one where I was forced to marry a man I didn't know and shipped off to another continent.

"I want you, Mason." My lips crashed down hard on his, not waiting for him to stop me or tell me how this was a terrible idea.

I didn't care that we'd barely talked or reconnected. Right now, in that very moment, I needed to feel safe. Mason was my safety net. He would catch me if I fell.

His mouth opened in kind, responding to the kiss, his hand pulling me tighter against his body. Warm, strong hands slid beneath my thick sweatshirt. His gentle touch grazed my bare skin.

I shuddered as he caressed my back, need outweighing everything else.

"Are you sure this is what you want?" Mason asked between feverish kisses.

"Yes," I said, staring deep into his gaze.

He lifted me into his arms and carried me to the bed, laying me down. He crawled up the mattress, straddled me, and hovered above my body. In haste, I tugged at his shirt, pulling it up and over his head.

Mason leaned down, whispering into my ear. "Do you realize you could get me fired doing this with a client?"

Staring up at him, I wrapped my legs around him, pulling him down, needing to feel his weight crush me, protect me, and make me whole—need outweighing everything else. I had no good answer other than I wanted him.

Was that enough? My fingers fumbled at the button on his jeans, and my hands trembled as I struggled to undo the metal.

"Hazel?" His fingers held mine in his hands. He sat on my hips, straddling me, before pinning my arms to the sides.

"I just—I need you, Mason." I sounded desperate. He'd probably call in one of his buddies to take over and never want to see me again.

"Maybe we should slow down." He pulled back and climbed off my body.

I whimpered before I realized the sound that slipped out past my throat. He'd done that to me, made me feel things I thought were impossible.

I didn't want to slow down or stop. Breathing hard, gasping for air, I lay staring up at the ceiling.

Mason climbed off the mattress, fixing his jeans button which I had managed to unclasp but not unzip. He grabbed his shirt from the bed and put his top back on.

Mason cleared his throat. "Ariella will be back soon, and we can't be caught in a compromising position."

Was that his concern, that we'd be caught by his colleagues?

I sat up and hurried to the bathroom, slamming the door shut on my heel. I slid down along the door, my back against the cold wood as I sat on the floor, my knees pulled up to my chest.

Regret filled my heart. I'd been foolish to think we could pick up where we'd left off.

Time seemed to trickle by like sand in an hourglass, one grain at a time.

Without my phone handy or a clock nearby, I didn't know how long I spent on the floor.

A firm knock vibrated through the wooden door. "You all right in there?" Mason asked.

"Fine." I would be after all of this was over and Franco left me alone. I didn't know how that would ever be possible unless I was put into witness protection or given a new identity—the types of arrangements that were made in movies for innocent victims.

I wasn't innocent.

My hands were covered in blood, the same as Nikolai's.

CHAPTER ELEVEN

MASON

I'd never met anyone more confusing in my life.

Hazel had stolen my heart and my virginity in high school. We'd been each other's first and vowed to only love each other forever.

It had been a fantasy, an empty promise that neither of us kept after we had graduated high school.

I'd gone into the military. Hazel had gone across the country to college, somewhere out west.

When or why she returned to Chicago, I wasn't certain. In fact, I didn't even know with absolute certainty that she left Chicago as she had intended.

It would be a lie to say that I never thought about her. I found myself comparing other women to her constantly. She had been the one who got away—the woman I loved and let escape.

I hadn't chased her. Maybe I should have.

With time, I assumed we'd grown apart. We were two different people than when we knew each other back at boarding school.

She'd had that predatory look in her eyes when Ariella left the two of us alone.

I hadn't thought anything of it at first. I'd assumed she'd watch television, and I'd make sure that Franco didn't find out where she stayed.

I hadn't wanted to stop, with her pert little body tucked tight under my hips.

I could have spent hours memorizing every curve and tasting every inch of her skin. I wanted to discover her all over again, see if she was just the way I remembered her.

We couldn't let desire interfere and risk her life. I needed to be alert, keeping an eye on the room or anything suspicious happening nearby. It was hard to do that while my lips were locked with hers.

Her soft lips still sent tingles throughout my entire body.

I needed a cold shower, but that was out of the question.

Instead, I'd gotten the cold shoulder. She'd locked herself in the bathroom for nearly an hour.

Ariella would be back from the store any minute.

Did Hazel wait for Ariella to return so that she wouldn't have to be alone with me and face me after what happened?

I approached the bathroom door, my hand perched on the wood. I gave a soft rap. "You all right in there?" I asked.

I wasn't expecting her to have an issue with Franco or need me for anything that she couldn't handle on her own in the bathroom. I was just trying for a basic conversation starter, a way to get her to retreat from her hiding place.

"Fine."

Any woman who ever told me she was 'fine' was never all right. I'd learned repeatedly that 'fine' was a code word for 'leave me the fuck alone' or 'it's all your fault.'

I wasn't sure how this was my fault other than I'd stopped us from going any further. While we were two consenting adults, I also didn't think it was wise for Ariella to walk in on us hot and sweaty between the sheets.

I wasn't one to kiss and tell, let alone let the new girl at the office pay witness to our cravings.

I held up my hand to knock again, but that seemed counterproductive. If she wanted to come out of the bathroom, she could join me.

I let my hand fall to my side and dug out my cell phone, glancing at the messages briefly before putting it on the table. There wasn't anything timely or important that came through.

I slumped back into the chair, my attention on the door as I waited for Ariella to return.

Hazel would undoubtedly come out of the bathroom when Ariella returned. Right?

Twenty minutes later, Ariella had arrived with several shopping bags of clothes and toiletries for Hazel.

Hazel wouldn't look at me as the two women sat perched on the bed, going through the contents of the bags.

I sat in the corner of the room, observing the two of them. It was almost as if I didn't exist.

Ariella glanced up at me and gave me a smile before returning her attention back to Hazel.

Well, I wasn't invisible at least.

"Do you want me to cut your hair and then color it?" Ariella asked.

Hazel looked distraught, her eyes wide and skin ghastly. "I knew I'd have to do this. I'm just not ready yet."

"I promise I'll make your hair look good, and no one will recognize you. We can chop off several inches, and with a bombshell blonde, no one will think twice it's you," Ariella said.

"I hope so."

"Come with me." Ariella brought the shearing scissors into the bathroom.

Hazel stalled for a long moment, her attention on the floor. She wouldn't so much as look at me.

When this was all over and Hazel was safe, the two of us needed to have a long talk.

"Are you coming?" Ariella asked.

Hazel meandered to the bathroom and then abruptly shut the door. I could hear chatter, and then the bathroom fan turned on, probably to drown out any discussion of me.

Had Ariella noticed the shift in mood with Hazel? I tried not to give any impression things had changed over the past hour while she'd been away.

The fire alarm emitted its ear-piercing squeal—the white light flashed inside the hotel room. I pulled out my gun, prepared for whatever happened next.

Stalking toward the bathroom and the room's exit, I gave a firm knock on the bathroom door.

"We hear it," Ariella said. She pulled open the bathroom door. It didn't appear that she'd started on cutting Hazel's hair. At least I didn't notice any recognizable difference.

"Put your hood back up," I commanded. With my gun drawn, I grabbed the handle to the door and carefully stepped out into the hallway.

Smoke filled the corridor.

"Stay close." I led the way with Ariella at the back and Hazel sandwiched between us.

My eyes burned with smoke, and I held my breath.

Fits of coughing erupted from behind. I couldn't turn around to see if it was Hazel or Ariella struggling to breathe.

"Keep moving. We're almost at the exit." I had studied the exit from our hotel room. We had to pass three doors before I reached the door to the stairwell.

Through the blinding smoke, my eyes burned and teared.

I felt for the door, swung it open, and was relieved the stairwell was smoke free.

"Come on!" I shouted for Ariella and Hazel. They were right at my feet, both of them hurrying down the stairs with me.

The floodlights to the stairs emitted a faint halogen glow. The bulbs flickered, spitting out enough light to illuminate the path.

I secured my gun, not wanting to alarm any of the guests as they poured out from each floor, the stairwell becoming more crowded as I kept Hazel behind Ariella and me tight to her back.

My boots trampled against the steps, and as I came to the first floor and followed the stream of guests out of the stairwell, my instincts took over.

Men with black ski masks and semi-automatic guns held hostages in the lobby.

"Turn that damned alarm off!" the man closest to me screamed. He waved the barrel aimlessly, threatening everyone but his buddies who had taken over the hotel.

"Get down!" another masked man shouted at us, his weapon poised at the guests coming down the stairwell. "On the ground, now!"

I gestured for Hazel and Ariella to get down.

"No secret signals." The masked man smashed the barrel of the weapon against my head, knocking me to my ass.

Blood dripped down my forehead. The gash burned, but not worse than my pride.

Doubled over, he searched me for a weapon, his semi-automatic pointed at my head. He shoved my gun into his dark black pants.

"Eagle Tactical, huh? You're coming with us."

CHAPTER TWELVE

ARIELLA

The smoke had been a diversion on the third floor to drive everyone out of their rooms and downstairs.

Who were the men with guns, and why had they assaulted Mason and taken him with them?

"I'll be fine," he said, glancing over his shoulder at us.

Crimson dripped to the linoleum floor, staining the hallway.

Mason was whisked out of the lobby.

I couldn't see where they took him. His hands were held up in the air, a sign of surrender. His weapon had been confiscated.

Did he have a backup gun?

Hazel's eyes glistened.

We lay on the floor near the stairwell, our hands on our heads. With my head turned, I faced Hazel, trying to convey that it would be okay.

The masked men, eight of them whom I had counted when we were first forced onto the ground, searched all of us as we lay on the floor, stealing away phones, keys, anything that could be used as a weapon or to call for help.

The fire alarm shut off.

Someone had pulled the fire alarm.

The fire department would be required to respond to the call and would notify the police when they saw what they were up against.

Thick metal chains secured the doors shut from the inside. We couldn't leave, not without someone escorting us out of the building.

My breathing hitched, and a wave of nausea coursed through my body. I needed to get ahold of my emotions and settle the fear that pumped into my veins.

I shut my eyes and counted to ten. I practiced my biofeedback breathing exercises to calm my heart rate, which would help settle my nerves too. I imagined a black nothingness with a single wave. With each breath, I followed the wave and inhaled slowly, held it, then exhaled at the same speed.

The tremor in my hand was minimal, but the exercise kept my entire body from shaking.

"Everyone, against the wall!" the masked man demanded of us. "Slowly! No sudden movements or we will shoot you."

He pointed the gun into the ceiling and blasted a round of bullets, instilling fear, reminding us that they were in charge and to do as instructed.

Hazel and I sat up and scooted back against the wall.

Where had they taken Mason?

Clearly, they'd known him. Which meant it had to be someone local, right?

Had they known Mason had been staying at the hotel? He hadn't checked in to the resort, so someone would have had to see him or his vehicle outside.

Unless it had nothing to do with Mason, and they just wanted to remove him out of the equation.

It was no secret that he was former military special forces and would lay his life on the line to protect everyone else.

Without him, what chance did we have to get out of this alive?

Of the eight masked men I'd noticed earlier, there were only six now. Where had the other two gone? One had taken Mason out of the room. Had I miscounted?

Hazel reached for my hand. I gave it a squeeze, wanting to reassure her that we would be okay. Her grip tightened against my palm. I glanced at her, frozen in fear, her eyes trained across the room at two men in suits on the floor held hostage with us.

"Them," she whispered so that only I could hear her.

"You know them?" I asked.

"That's Franco," Hazel whispered. She hung her head, letting the hoodie fall over her eyes.

Had the men recognized her? I didn't want to make it obvious that I'd spotted them.

Casually, I glanced around the room at everyone, mentally taking note of the number of hostages, how many were children, whether anyone was injured, and then let my gaze study the men who wanted Hazel.

They were talking amongst one another, their backs pressed against the wall. They looked like two giant thugs, dark hair, lots of muscle in dark suits.

They were too far away for me to hear what the two men said to one another. Maybe that was a good thing if they hadn't noticed Hazel nestled beside me.

I was her last chance of protection.

I didn't have a weapon, and there were masked men with guns watching our every move.

How were we going to get out of this alive?

CHAPTER THIRTEEN

MASON

Darkness surrounded my vision.

The man who had dragged me out of the hotel and into the back of a dark van shoved a hood over my head and bound my arms behind my back with zip ties.

He said nothing.

Was he concerned if he spoke again that I would recognize his voice?

He knew who I worked for, which meant he knew me.

The door slammed shut. I listened and waited for another door to slam. It didn't happen. The engine didn't hum to life, either.

A click from across the parking lot. Was it a door shutting? Had the offender gone back into the building?

I'd been alone in the white unmarked van that had been parked near the side exit of the resort. I needed to remove the binds from my wrists, and then I'd deal with the bastards who had taken over Blue Sky Resort.

What were they after, money? The hotel probably didn't have much cash on hand, as booking a hotel room always required using a credit card, but it was possible cash was exchanged for ski and snowboard rental equipment.

I'd seen eight men in masks, all in dark clothes and black pants, with matching black shoes.

They didn't want anyone to recognize them, but they knew me. Which meant I knew them. Whoever they were, they were amateurs.

I bent forward and used my body to create as much space as possible. I'd trained for this, and while I could have done the motion while in the hotel, I was outmanned and outgunned. I slammed down my arms, breaking the zip ties.

I yanked the hood off my head and tossed it to the floor before I opened the door of the truck and stepped out. That was too easy.

Sirens wailed in the distance, coming closer.

A fire engine and police car pulled into the parking lot.

An ambulance trailed in the distance.

The sheriff stopped in front of the building and stepped out, his lights left on but the siren silent. "I didn't expect to see you twice in one day, Reid. Can you tell me what's going on? The fire alarm went off, but no one is outside."

Even he recognized the huge red flag. "Hostage situation, eight offenders with semi-automatics. They're holed up in the lobby with hostages."

I reached for my phone in my pocket to discover it wasn't there. I'd left it on the table upstairs.

Shit.

I needed to contact the team.

"Did they tell you what they wanted? Any demands?" Sheriff Nelson asked.

"Nothing. They knew I was with Eagle Tactical. One of them coldcocked me with his gun, stole my weapon, and dragged my ass outside. He threw me in the back of the van. Lucky for me, he only had zip ties and not handcuffs." Handcuffs were a hell of a lot harder to break free from.

"Locals. Did you recognize any of their voices?" Sheriff Nelson asked.

"No." I wished I could have been of more help.

"Do you have any guys inside?"

"Two, but they're not my brothers. The new girl we hired and a client. Neither have special forces training like my buddies."

I wanted it clear that they were not in a position to stop what happened on the inside.

Sheriff Nelson called for backup and then contacted Eagle Tactical for their expertise.

This is what we trained for, and while we weren't always the ones charging into danger, with our combined years of experience, we were always available for consultations in the field.

Emma stepped outside the side door, a box of cigarettes in hand.

"Stop right there! Hands up!" Sheriff Nelson blasted into the loudspeaker attached to his squad car.

She dropped her lighter and box of cigarettes to the ground. Eyes wide, she held up her hands and took a slow step back, reached for the door, and flung herself back inside the building.

The door slammed shut behind her.

"Call Declan," I said. "Tell him to run everything he can on Emma Foster."

"Wait, you know her?" Sheriff Nelson asked. "Is she your client? The one who's inside with your new girl?"

"No. Emma recently moved to Breckenridge. We ran her background when she was hired by the resort as part of their hiring practice. She came up clean."

Why did she come back to Breckenridge? It was clear she was helping the men who had taken over the building. And the fact she'd been hanging out with the off-gridders and living with them, what the hell were they after?

Sheriff Nelson tossed me his cell phone. I called Declan at the office, relayed the information about Emma to him. As I hung up the phone, Jaxson and Aiden pulled into the parking lot.

"Looks like the rest of your team is here," the sheriff said.

Aiden climbed out of the truck and glanced me over. "How's your head? Do you need to get checked out by paramedics?"

"My head is fine." Since when had he taken on Jaxson's role of being the parent to the team? I expected it from Jaxson, especially since he was a father. "My ego got a little bruised, that's all."

Getting my ass dragged out in front of the town couldn't have helped our image at Eagle Tactical. I should have fought harder and knocked that guy with the gun on his ass.

"I'm sure you'll recover. Hazel and Ariella are inside?"

"Unfortunately. Where's Jaxson?" I asked.

"He'll be out in a minute. He's on the phone talking to our client's brother. It turns out he's requesting information since he can't get ahold of Franco."

My head spun. "What? He's trying to hire us now too?" What were the odds? It wasn't like we were located in Chicago and they both had searched for a private security firm.

"No. Franco had given our contact information to Nikolai in case he didn't check in with him," Aiden said. "Any chance these guys are the ones from the restaurant this morning?"

"The two deceased men were Alexander Petrov and Miko Romanoff," I said.

Jaxson slammed the door of the truck as he stomped over toward us, fuming.

Was his shitty mood a result of the phone call or the fact he'd been sexually frustrated the past few days working alongside Ariella? There wasn't much more

I could take of his attitude. I shot a glance at Declan. He saw it too, didn't he?

Declan gave a faint nod and then rubbed at his jaw, glancing at the resort. "How many armed men did you see?" Declan asked.

"There were eight in the lobby, armed with semi-automatic weapons and wearing ski-masks. I didn't see any body armor, which is good news for us," I said.

Another officer brought over a map of the facility and spread it out over the hood of the squad car.

I pointed at the exit that Emma had come in and out of easily. "This appears to be the only point of an entrance that isn't locked." I had noticed metal chains on the doors before being pistol-whipped. I'd tried to take in as much detail as possible. I was the only eyes the team had right now.

"SWAT is on their way. I'd like Eagle Tactical to assist," the sheriff said, "but we're in charge of the operation."

"Of course," I said. "We wouldn't have it any other way." We knew how procedure worked on these types of cases. There was often red tape involved, and they couldn't just hand over the reins for us to take the lead.

"Where are Ariella and Hazel?" Jaxson asked.

I swallowed the lump in my throat. Had they not gotten the news from the sheriff?

"They're inside the resort." I met his icy stare, unwilling to cower.

His gaze tightened. "I realize that. Where in the building were they last located?"

I pointed on the map where we had been. By now, it was likely they'd been moved someplace else. "Here."

"How many hostages were inside?" the sheriff asked.

I hadn't been able to count fast enough the total number. I could give a rough estimate. "Fifty hostages, maybe sixty-five." There hadn't been too many people who had filtered in down the stairs while I'd been getting my head smashed in by the barrel of a gun.

"We'll start with negotiations and see what they want," Jaxson said.

"There's something you should know, Jaxson." He glanced from the map of the building back up at me. "We believe Emma may be involved in the hostage takeover. She came outside to take a smoke."

"I don't get it. Why not just smoke inside the building if she's involved?" Jaxson's brow furrowed, his jaw tight.

I didn't have an answer or an explanation for him, at least not yet. Maybe I was wrong. Maybe she heard the fire alarm and had been locked in a bathroom and then stepped outside for a cigarette. Except why else would she have fled back inside the building at the first sign of the authorities?

She had to be hiding something.

Declan folded his arms across his chest. "Was she coming outside to see if anyone was coming to intervene? I don't know Emma, but this doesn't sound like what I know of her."

I snorted under my breath. "She was with the off-gridders just last week."

"That doesn't make her guilty of a crime," Declan said, "just poor taste in friends."

"It does when she has a gun trained on Jaxson." I'd kept Jaxson's secret from Ariella, but I hadn't even considered mentioning it to the team. Should I have said something sooner? I ran a hand through my hair. It was too late now to second guess that decision. I couldn't make another mistake, not with so many lives at risk.

"Ariella doesn't know Emma's involved with the off-gridders," Jaxson said. "Means they could be using her to get to us."

Would they go that far? "Did she call you or try to communicate with you?" I asked Jaxson. Those two had been close, and while right now there'd been an obvious tiff of sorts, she still would have gone to him if she was in trouble, right?

"No. I texted her, but she didn't respond. Declan pinged her phone and said it's turned off," Jaxson said.

"They probably took everyone's phones," I said. "Hostage takeover 101."

"Thank you for that." Jaxson shook his head and stormed toward the truck.

"Where are you going?" I followed him as he opened the trunk and retrieved our tactical equipment.

Jaxson retrieved a bulletproof vest and put it on over his shirt.

"I refuse to sit on my ass and wait for SWAT to tell us how to do our job, or worse, the town sheriff. Are you coming with me?"

CHAPTER FOURTEEN

ARIELLA

With my back pressed against the cold brick, I tucked my knees to my chest.

Hazel sat to my right, pressed tight against my body as we were crammed together in the lobby.

I'd trained with the C.I.A. on how to take out an assailant in a hostage takeover, but there wasn't a class that involved eight armed men versus a tech operative.

I'd never had any exciting field opportunities. I'd sat in hotel rooms in foreign countries listening with surveillance equipment. That had been the extent of my excitement.

This went beyond that, and quite honestly, I could have done without the thrill. I didn't like high-adrenaline adventures, and this one was making my heart hammer in my chest.

Having autonomic dysfunction sucked on a normal day. Today, it really wreaked havoc on me. It took every ounce of strength to force my body to stay calm, to not tremble even though the fight-or-flight reflex had taken over.

My breathing exercises sucked. Biofeedback was a great tool with the right equipment. Seated on the floor with masked men threatening us with guns was not the right time to use it.

I wished I would have had a weapon. Although what good would it have done? I wasn't likely capable of stopping eight men, maybe one or two on a good day. Six had stayed with us, and the other two who had disappeared returned, but Mason wasn't with them.

Where was he? Was he alive? Had they tortured him?

I tried to think of anything else. Puppies. Summer sunsets. Surfing at the beach. Jaxson. The last one brought a faint quirk to my lips and it made my stomach flop.

I hadn't wanted to think about him.

The man Hazel was afraid of cleared his throat. "How much longer are you going to keep us? Some of us have business to attend to."

He had a heavy accent, definitely Russian. I'd studied languages as part of my curriculum at the C.I.A..

The shortest of the masked men stormed over to the Russian and shoved the barrel of the gun into his chest, poised against his heart. "You'll shut up!" the masked man barked.

"Or what? You'll shoot me?" the Russian snorted a laugh, unfazed by the threat. However, he didn't physically fight back. "You don't scare me. I've killed cockroaches bigger than you."

"That's Franco," Hazel whispered into my ear.

She'd mentioned that earlier, but I hadn't known which one he was until now.

There were two greasy-haired thick men in suits who sat on the floor against the opposite wall.

If the bastard shot Franco, he'd be unknowingly doing all of us a favor.

"You may not be afraid of death, but what about if I kill your friend?" The masked man moved the barrel of the gun away from Franco's chest to the other man's head. "I'm itching to pull the trigger."

"Go ahead and do it," Franco said. He sounded bored.

Was it some form of reverse psychology?

I couldn't see the masked man's eyes from across the room. We all watched. A heaviness fell over the room. Several soft gasps of fear from hostages spilled out.

"Enough!" A larger man wearing a mask and waving a gun pushed the barrel away from the man's head.

He grabbed the shorter man by the arm and dragged him down the hallway.

"Coward!" Franco shouted.

My hands trembled as I expelled a nervous breath. The men holding us captive weren't murderers. At least not yet.

What were they doing taking hostages at the resort? What could they possibly hope to achieve?

One of the masked men whisked a woman, her hands bound behind her back, toward us. "Let me go!" her voice carried down the hallway.

Emma?

Her long brown hair covered her red, splotchy cheeks and eyes. Had she been crying?

"Leave me alone!" Emma slipped away from the masked man's grasp and landed her gaze on me.

She sniffled and collapsed onto the floor in a heap at my side.

"Did they hurt you?" I asked, my voice hardly above a whisper.

The masked man lifted the handle of his weapon and pointed it at my forehead. "Quiet!" he snarled.

Trembling, I lowered my gaze. I didn't want to appear threatening. The last thing we needed was garnering Franco's attention and him noticing Hazel beside me.

"Smart girl," he said with a laugh. I imagined a dark and sinister smile behind those icy blue eyes.

His voice sent a shiver down my spine. It was rough and thick. He snorted and lowered the gun but bent down to grab my arm.

"You're coming with me." He yanked me to my feet, his grip tight and hard, unforgiving.

"No!" I pulled back from his grasp.

I was safer with the other hostages. I didn't trust the masked man, what he might make me do with him.

"You don't tell me no," he seethed and jerked my hair, his fist tangling the strands as he pulled my neck back to face him.

Were all eyes on us? I couldn't look away, my neck twisted to stare only up at the man's face, the mask making it impossible for me to see him.

He hoisted me over his shoulder and, with his other hand, grabbed Hazel's arm. She at least had a thick sweatshirt to protect her from his tight grip.

"Let me go!" I fought with all my strength. My hands punched at his lower back, pounding into him. It was worthless. He wore a vest beneath his black shirt, thick, like Kevlar, concealable.

"Shut it or I put a bullet in both of your heads!"

CHAPTER FIFTEEN

JAXSON

Mason grabbed a pair of bolt cutters, and we breached the side entrance of the resort. Sitting around and waiting for SWAT to negotiate wasn't going to work.

I'd gotten a call from Nikolai Agron, the last person I wanted to deal with today.

If everything I'd heard was true, then I'd taken on a client I wasn't comfortable handling. I had dealt with men who were scumbags in the past, but this was different.

I usually had the upper hand.

I didn't like that Ariella and Hazel were being held hostage, and Franco was nowhere to be found. The actions at the resort didn't reflect the mafia's strategies. Had Franco known Hazel had booked a room, he would have undoubtedly snatched her or killed her, depending on his desires.

I wasn't sure which he had planned. While he'd wanted her as his wife, the fact he'd gunned the marshals down and hadn't thought twice about her safety made me suspect that he was prepared to kill her. Was it because she betrayed him?

I gestured at Mason to follow me down the hall. He gave a curt nod and covered me from behind. Guns were drawn; we hugged the wall as we came around the corner. In the distance, voices grew louder, more prominent. That meant we were close.

Her mousy brown hair had been chopped recently into a bob cut. Emma Foster, the birth mother of my daughter, stood just around the corner to another hallway with a vending machine.

Dressed in her black slacks and blue-collared resort shirt, she tapped her foot against the linoleum floor. "I don't see why I couldn't have worn a mask and dressed up with you guys," Emma said.

Just on the other side of the vending machine, was a masked man. His gun poked out from behind the appliance as he stepped forward.

Dressed all in black, he was the same height and build as I was. I could easily take him, but not with Emma watching.

Emma was definitely involved.

Had she known what was going down? How big a part did she play? Did she orchestrate the entire situation? I had a plethora of questions, but they wouldn't get answered if I approached her. That wasn't how she worked, not with me. There was a history between us, a complicated one.

We weren't friends. We weren't even lovers. We'd spent one night together, technically one very long day, and that had been it.

The masked man leaned into Emma and whispered something into her ear before she stammered off down the hall.

I waited until Emma was out of sight and rounded the corner before the masked man could anticipate that anyone had been watching them. I rammed into his body, throwing him off balance.

He stumbled backward, tripping over his feet, his gun falling to the floor out of his grasp. I held my breath. Had Emma heard the ruckus? Would she come back and find the two of us fighting?

Mason stood guard, watching my back.

I snatched the weapon from the ground and pointed it at the masked man. "Take it off," I seethed between clenched teeth. There was only one way in, and that was dressed like them.

"Bite me," the masked man said and smacked his forehead against mine.

Fuck, that hurt. I swallowed the pain as he struggled for the gun in my hands. No. I wouldn't give it to him. I stomped on his foot, elbowed his stomach, and kneed his groin.

Playing dirty was the only way to survive. We weren't in a boxing ring playing by a set of predetermined rules. This was life or death.

"Bastard," he grunted and lunged at me, slamming my back against the brick wall.

I gasped from the impact, and Mason hurried closer, gun drawn and poised on the masked man's forehead.

I thrust his mask off, shocked.

Jayden Scott. He'd been running with the off-gridders for too long.

"What the hell?" I couldn't believe what he'd gotten himself involved in. We'd served in the special forces together and were brothers. It felt like a lifetime ago when I stared back at his cold gaze.

Was his involvement because of Emma? They'd seemed pretty chummy together near the vending machines earlier. Had that been why he'd shown up?

I handed Mason the semi-automatic as he stood behind me. I didn't need Jayden getting his dirty claws on it again.

With one hand gripping Jayden's black shirt, I shoved my pistol against his head. "Give me one reason I shouldn't unload the magazine," I said between gritted teeth.

"You don't know anything," Jayden said.

"Why are you here? What do they want?" Men don't show up and take hostages for sport, certainly not these men, off-gridders.

What were they after? I shoved my face in his, the safety off—my index finger on the trigger. I was ready to shoot him, a man whose life I'd saved a decade ago.

He snorted and shrugged. Jayden didn't so much as sweat with the barrel against his skin. "You don't have it in you to shoot me, Monroe."

I hated how well he knew me. The truth was I wouldn't shoot an unarmed man unless my life was in mortal danger. It wasn't, at least not right now, but everyone else's lives were.

I had no other choice. I took the handle of the gun and slammed it against his head, knocking him unconscious. He fell to the ground in a heap.

"Help me get his clothes off him," I said.

Mason stood there, shouldering one gun while keeping the other pointed around the corner, prepared at a moment's notice to protect us. "Looks like you got it handled."

Sighing, I stripped Jayden down to his boxers. I didn't feel good about what I did, but what other choice was there?

Two of us against eight, with dozens of hostages, didn't bode well. At least it was seven now, except Emma was involved.

I needed to take her out of the equation.

I opened the nearest door, a janitorial supply closet, and dragged Jayden inside. I shut the door, and with Mason's help, we quickly dragged the vending machine in front to block Jayden from escaping. Just in case he woke up before my plan was complete.

Quick to don Jayden's clothes, I slid on the last part of the ensemble, the black ski mask, and held out my hand for the gun that Mason had been watching for me.

"You sure about this?" Mason asked. "You're a father. Maybe I should be the one risking my life."

It seemed he had second thoughts. I couldn't allow myself to second guess any decisions now or in the future. "I got this."

I needed to protect Ariella as well as Hazel. My job involved risking my life. It was part of the position.

On my belt, were a handful of zip ties that Jayden had worn on his pants. While I didn't intend on taking hostages, I also couldn't let Emma discover I wasn't Jayden.

Would she recognize my voice or my eyes through the mask? We may have only spent one night together, but she'd shown up at my door with Isabella, and I'd shown up at her door telling her to leave town a little over a month ago.

I gestured for Mason to follow me down the hallway. Emma stayed away from the hostages. She leaned against the wall, her phone in hand, staring down at the device, oblivious to my presence.

Mason hung back, watching with his gun drawn in case I needed backup.

I snuck up without her so much as flinching.

Her focus was entirely on the game she was playing on her cell phone, which involved a series of colorful bubbles that made no sense to me.

I grabbed her arms and thrust them behind her back. Her phone fell to the floor.

Yanking a zip tie, I secured her wrists, binding them together.

"Jayden," Emma's voice held a hint of annoyance. "This isn't funny. Let me go."

I didn't answer her. I didn't want to speak yet, worried she might recognize my voice wasn't *his*.

I had to be careful. I may have had only one chance, and I didn't want to ruin it before I found Ariella and Hazel.

It took all my strength not to turn around and glance at Mason. I was used to sharing signals in the field. He had my back. I had to trust that he had it now, too, while I couldn't turn around.

"Fine. If you want to play cops and robbers, I guess I can play along." Emma almost sounded bored.

The mask was hot, stuffy. I breathed heavily through my nose, doing everything I could to keep my mouth shut. It was difficult. I wanted to tell her to shut up. To shake her and demand to know what the hell she'd gotten herself involved with and why.

What sane person would leave their life behind to live amongst the off-gridders? Their refuge was a hell hole, compromised of a commune with no running water or heat. They were basic, lived off the land, and depended on each other for survival.

It might have been a nice idea if they weren't men with sinister pasts.

I still had yet to grasp what they wanted, why they'd taken over the Blue Sky Resort. I couldn't flat out ask Emma. It would alert her that I wasn't Jayden.

I grabbed her elbow and escorted her with heavy footsteps toward the crowd of noise and commotion. Mostly, it involved tears and whispered pleas, some praying, others talking amongst one another.

The offenders hadn't demanded silence. Okay, so they weren't worried about being overthrown or the hostages working together to defeat them.

If the perpetrators were all off-gridders, then these weren't the brightest men. Some had military training, but not all. Most who had served would have been dishonorably discharged.

These weren't honorable men.

I led Emma down the hall and glanced from one person to the next until my gaze landed on Ariella.

She rocked slowly, her knees pressed tight to her chest, her arms wrapped around her legs. To her right, was a hostage with an oversized sweatshirt, hood up.

I'd recognize that hoodie anywhere. It belonged to Mason Reid. It must have been Hazel buried underneath, which was probably wise.

I briefly glanced at the hostages. A few were town folk, the owners of the resort, and several guests I didn't know. They'd have to wait. Hazel was my priority, and Ariella. I refused to leave her behind.

"Leave me alone!" Emma pulled away from me, sniffled, and fell to the ground beside Ariella. She knew how to play the part of the victim. How long had she been auditioning for that role?

"Did they hurt you?" Ariella whispered, falling for her performance.

I hated watching Ariella filled with fear, trembling against the wall, but I had to make it convincing if I wanted everyone to believe I was one of them.

I had no other choice. I lifted the handle of my gun and poised it at her forehead. "Quiet!" I barked out orders.

The shiver coursed through her body. Anyone could see the fear I had instilled in her.

No. I had to separate the two. I was only here to save her. These men had caused her trauma. "Smart girl," I said and tried my damnedest to laugh.

I needed to be convincing, or I'd put all of our lives in danger. I lowered my gun and bent down to grab her arm. "You're coming with me." I hoisted Ariella to her feet.

"No!"

She was a fighter; I'd give her that. "You don't tell me no," I seethed. I had no choice but to demand her to come, show force. These men wouldn't take no so easily.

I grabbed a fistful of her hair and jerked her head back to face me.

I stared into her eyes, filled with fright. Could she see me? Did she recognize my eyes through the ski mask?

I wanted to tell her to trust me, but I couldn't. Her fear is what made it believable to everyone who watched us.

I couldn't risk Ariella fighting me. I needed to demand Hazel to come with me too. It was the only way to save them. Hopefully, Ariella would understand and forgive me when she saw it was me beneath the mask.

I tossed her over my shoulder and grabbed Hazel's arm, thrusting her up onto her feet.

"Let me go!" Ariella shrieked.

She was strong for her tiny frame, her fists landing blow after blow at my lower back. Truthfully, it didn't hurt. The vest did a decent job of shielding me from her assault.

Had she discovered who was beneath the mask?

I needed to sound convincing. I had to get us past the other armed men. "Shut it, or I put a bullet in both of your heads!"

Hazel was the least of all to fight me. Her body was limp, but my grip on her arm made sure that she didn't slip from my grasp.

I stalked with them back the way we came, past the hostages, including two men on my right in suits, legs spread out, seated on the floor. Our eyes locked. *Franco Ivanov*.

I whisked the girls past the throes of people.

"Where are you taking them?" another male voice answered. He stood twenty feet away, masked and armed.

"Put me down," Ariella grunted. She continued to pound against my back, but her motions felt less forceful. Was it for show, or had she felt defeated?

"For some filthy fun. I thought I'd teach them each a lesson for disobeying us." Bile rose to my throat. I wanted to vomit.

The masked man scoffed and turned on his heel, not entirely interested in me or my plans.

I carried them down the hall, turned, and shoved Hazel into Mason's arms.

Mason held up a finger to his lips to be quiet. He grabbed Hazel's hand and whisked her down the corridor, out the direction we came in.

"I won't let you!" Ariella continued to fight me. With her head bent down, she'd failed to see Mason helping Hazel. "Fight him!" she shouted to Hazel.

I kept my pace, falling behind Mason and Hazel as they jogged down the hall for the entrance that we'd come in from.

I wanted to tell Ariella that it was me, but I couldn't risk anyone discovering us.

What if another masked man caught up with us, or worse, Jayden had freed himself?

CHAPTER SIXTEEN

ARIELLA

I squirmed against his shoulder, and while the masked man had kept an arm around my hips, I didn't stop my movements. He'd grow tired or be forced to put me down and I'd have the chance to fight back. It was just the two of us.

His grip loosened just slightly, and I used all my strength to roll hard against him, knocking him over and us onto the floor.

A male voice grunted, "Damnit, Freckles."

It couldn't be. Could it? "Jaxson?" I whispered.

I probably should have run. It was my opportunity, but I'd recognize that voice anywhere when it said my name.

He glanced over his shoulder as he stood up, dusted off his pants, and offered me a hand.

Those piercing blue eyes stole my heart. I clutched his hand, and we tore out of the building.

SWAT awaited our departure out of the building. Guns pointed at us.

I threw my arms into the air.

Jaxson did the same. The shotgun was slung over his shoulder. He fell to his knees, the mask still on as SWAT surrounded him.

"Don't shoot!" I screamed at the men. "He's with Eagle Tactical." I had assumed they'd sent him in as part of their operation.

"Even more reason to arrest his ass," a man with a SWAT jacket said.

He stepped out from behind the command center positioned across the parking lot. He must have been the leader of the operation.

"Jaxson?" What the hell was going on?

———

SWAT agents patted me down to make sure I wasn't harboring a weapon before they whisked me away from Jaxson.

"I want to see Jaxson," I demanded. Why were they keeping us apart? "He saved my life." I insisted that they know he rescued me.

Was it the fact he was dressed as one of *them* that they had to check out his story?

Had he broken the rules coming in to rescue Hazel and me? Where was Hazel? Worry flooded my face as I sat in a metal folding chair, a blanket around my shoulders.

"Relax," Mason said, coming to sit beside me. He handed me a bottle of water. "Jaxson said you might need this."

"Thank you."

Hazel stood behind him. She was small in comparison, and I hadn't even realized how easily she disappeared. He was her protector.

Had he been inside the resort too? I hadn't seen him, but that didn't mean anything. Eagle Tactical worked as a team.

I doubted Jaxson had gone in alone.

"Where is he?" I asked. I opened the bottle of water and took a sip. I used two hands to hold the bottle, doing my best to keep my hands from shaking. The blanket helped, even though I didn't feel cold. I didn't feel much of anything other than exhausted.

"Debriefing and dealing with the repercussions of what we did," Mason said. He wrapped an arm around Hazel, pulling her tight against his body.

"I don't understand. Is he in trouble?"

Mason smirked, chill. "No more than usual. I need to get Hazel someplace safe. She mentioned Franco was inside the resort. I can't risk waiting around for him to find us out here."

"Yes, that's right." She couldn't stay at the hotel anymore. I didn't dare ask where he'd take her. I wasn't sure I wanted to know. It was best to keep it a secret from everyone.

He rested a hand on my shoulder. "Are you sure you're all right? If I take you with us, Jaxson will lose his shit. He's just barely keeping it together," Mason said.

I sipped at my water and wiped my lips. "I'm fine. I doubt he wants to see me. He kicked me out of his place. I'm the last person he wants to deal with. Remember, I planned on staying at the hotel to get out of his hair."

"Talk to him," Mason said. He patted me on the back before leading Hazel out of the tent.

I wanted to leave. I didn't want to stay with the itchy blanket curled up over my shoulders, drinking a bottle of tepid water. I wanted to go home, slip into a hot bath, and let my troubles disappear.

————

Jaxson stormed into the tent, his shoulders heaving as he laid eyes on me. "Are you okay?"

He towered above me as I sat on the frigid metal chair. I pulled the blanket tighter, trying to ward off the cold. I shivered, but it was more from his proximity than the chill in the air.

I didn't answer, just stared up at him. Did he really care about how I was, or was this his protector mode that had him asking?

Earlier that morning, he didn't give a damn about me or my feelings. Why had that changed now?

"Just peachy," I said and gave the best smile I could muster.

He bent down. His knees flexed as he came to my eye level. "You're mad at me."

"What gave you that impression?" I shut my eyes and exhaled loudly before opening them again.

He didn't budge and continued to stare at me. "How about I drive you home? We're free to go."

Was he serious? He'd practically told me to find someplace else to live a few hours ago. Had he forgotten, or was he just feeling guilty that I'd been one of the victims?

"You don't have to feel sorry for me." I gently pushed at his chest to make him back up as I stood. "I'll be fine. I'm just going to find someplace else to stay." I wasn't sure what other options there were for accommodations, but I'd figure something out.

Maybe I could stay with Emma if she had a spare bedroom, or at least a couch I could crash on.

If not, maybe one of the other Eagle Tactical guys would suggest some place I could crash. I wasn't stupid enough to room with one of them. Jaxson would probably make their life hell.

"I don't feel sorry for you," he said and stood. He exhaled loudly and linked my arm with his. "I'm taking you home."

"Jaxson, I have my car. I can drive home." I wasn't really sure where I would go. Home didn't exist for me, not anymore.

"No." A single-word response.

He wasn't listening to me. Jaxson led me out of the tent and to his truck. He unlocked the door and helped me inside. I'd kept the blanket, putting it on my lap as I climbed into the front seat. "This isn't necessary. I'm capable of driving myself."

He waited until I buckled before he shut the door and jogged around to the opposite side. Jaxson climbed in, started the engine, and buckled his seatbelt. "I'm taking you home." His voice was firm and commanding.

Was he used to bossing people around? He'd been doing it the past few days at the office and mostly to me.

I took Mason's words into consideration that Jaxson was sexually frustrated, but that didn't even make sense. We'd had sex recently, and I was pretty sure he wasn't the kind of guy who slept around. He had a kid, and it had been obvious when we first met that he put her first.

I didn't answer, just stared out the side window as he drove us out of the parking lot and to the main thoroughfare, up to the mountain pass.

"I get it. You're mad at me," Jaxson said. The radio was off and the heat-blasted at full speed.

I glanced from the side window at Jaxson and then folded my arms across my chest.

"I'm sorry if I stepped over the line in there, but I couldn't let anything happen to you, Freckles."

"Don't!" I warned him. He didn't get to call me that name, not anymore.

We climbed the mountain, Jaxson downshifting the truck. The tires spun but just as quickly pulled us up the road.

His hands gripped the steering wheel hard. The roads didn't look that treacherous, but the higher we climbed in elevation, the more snow began to fall. At first, the flakes were thick and light and the road covered in a dusting, but it grew heavier with each passing minute.

"I didn't mean to hurt you," he said. "I had to look convincing that I was one of them."

I shifted in my seat and turned a bit to face him. "You think I'm mad about what happened in the resort?" He did what he needed to do so that he could get Hazel and me out of there.

He glanced briefly at me before returning his attention to the snow-covered terrain. "Aren't you?"

I laughed under my breath. "Gosh, you are clueless." Were all men this clueless?

"Gee, thanks," he muttered. He grumbled something incoherent under his breath.

I stared at him. "What was that?" I asked, daring him to say it aloud.

"I said, 'women, you all are the same.'"

"Who are you comparing me to, Emma?" I yanked at the blanket, my fingers tugging at the scratchy wool, clawing at it in fists. "You don't get to lump me in the same category as the woman who dropped off your kid and wanted nothing to do with her or you."

I grimaced after the words left my lips. That wasn't what I really thought of Emma but knowing what I did, the fact she'd never brought it up once, but Jaxson had told me, it nagged at me in the back of my mind.

Why was she here? Was she vying for his affection and attention?

I hadn't seen them together other than the one night at the bar, but maybe there was something I didn't know. I hadn't been in Breckenridge that long.

Had he been keeping his own secrets from me?

With one hand, he rubbed his forehead, and the other remained planted on the steering wheel. "I'm sorry."

"For what?" I didn't want him to apologize if he didn't mean it or he didn't know what for.

He stalled, not answering me right away.

"Here, I'll make it easy on you. You've been an ass to me, in fact, the biggest bosshole that I know of. Tell me I'm wrong," I said, staring at him.

He kept his focus on the road and every so often he glanced in my direction, but now he didn't look at me. He shifted under my gaze, clearly uncomfortable with what I'd said.

He wanted the truth. He deserved it.

His jaw was tight, his teeth clenched. His left hand came down on the steering wheel as he guided the truck onto the private driveway toward his residence.

"Yeah, that's what I thought. Don't worry. I'll be out of your hair as soon as I can find someplace to live. I had planned on staying at the resort, but it's under new management at the moment."

He huffed under his breath. "Do you think you're funny, cracking a joke like that? You could have gotten killed today."

"Well, I didn't. I'm sure you're disappointed that I'm still here, taking up residence under your roof." I hadn't intended to go so far, but the words slipped out. He didn't really wish me dead, right? He just hated me. Was there a difference? I pinched the bridge of my nose, feeling a headache coming on.

Maybe I should grab my blanket and steal a pillow and go sleep in the damned shed, the only piece of property I owned with a roof.

Well, it was that or my car, but my vehicle was down at the resort, which made sleeping in it hard. That would be my plan. I could easily live out of my car. I just needed to get back to the resort. It had to beat the death daggers Jaxson shot my way.

He shut off the vehicle and emitted a heavy sigh. I could feel the heat, the anger, the stress brooding in the truck. I didn't want to sit around and wait for him to erupt at me again.

I unlocked the truck door, thrust it open, and unbuckled myself. I spun my legs to the side to jump down when the blanket tangled around me.

Wrestling with it, I failed to notice Jaxson had hurried around the truck.

His body trapped mine, my legs tight, with him practically straddling me. His hands rested at each side of my hips against the truck's interior leather as he blocked me from escaping.

"We need to talk."

"There's nothing to talk about," I said and pushed at his chest to force him to move, but he was too strong.

His hands came up, clasping mine, crushing my hands against his chest, leaning closer.

"I don't think you mean that," Jaxson said.

I wouldn't look at him. I didn't want to give him any more of my time or attention. "I do," I said.

"I would never want anything to happen to you, Freckles." His right hand came up and stroked my jaw and guided my chin up to meet his stare. "I've been a jerk, but it's because I don't know how to do this," he said and gestured between us.

"Do what?"

"Be professional." He leaned his forehead against mine.

My eyes closed. I could smell the sweat against his skin mixed with the special scent that made him uniquely Jaxson.

His fingers tangled in the nape of my neck, bringing my lips closer. He held me in that position, not kissing me, just drinking in my breath, stealing my anger and pain as I felt need overtake us.

I wanted him, but I didn't want my heart broken. Not again. I couldn't handle it shattering into a million tiny pieces.

"This isn't professional," I whispered. My eyelids fluttered open, my gaze heavy. Each breath grew raspy and deep. I wanted him more than I had wanted anything in my life.

The worst of it was that I knew what I'd been missing. I'd had a taste of the forbidden fruit, and I wanted more.

"Screw professional." His lips latched onto mine, hard and forceful with need.

I clutched him tighter and pulled him to me, my fingers tangled in his hair as I drank him in. I wanted him, needed him, craved what only he could offer me.

"I'm sorry," he whispered, breaking the kiss, his lips, soft and warm, caressing my neck, sucking and nipping at the sensitive flesh.

I whimpered. He knew just what to do to make my knees weak. Thankfully, I was already seated. I dipped my head, and my fingers guided his lips back to mine, our tongues dueling for control, his body pressed tight against mine. I wanted him but was afraid to voice the words, not after what happened.

He pulled back slightly, and his lips trailed a warm, soft path to my ear. "I have something to tell you," he whispered.

"Don't want to talk," I said, dragging his mouth back down onto mine. Talking is what got us into trouble. It turned into fighting. This felt good, amazing, in fact, and made my head spin in a wonderful way.

Every fear that had flitted through my mind had vanished with his lips on mine.

"I left you a note the night I went home," he whispered, dropping soft butterfly kisses to my neck yet again.

I froze, my eyes wide, pulled from the sweet moment, and thrown back like a rubber band that snapped me to the reality of what happened.

"What?" I pulled back and put a hand between us to stop him. I needed to hear this, whatever he felt important enough to drop on me now.

"I didn't want to wake you when I left, so I scribbled you a note and stuck it to your new fridge. I'm guessing you never saw it." His eyes twinkled, and as I stared into the deep blue abyss, I could see he spoke the truth.

Jaxson wasn't a man who would lie to save himself.

I didn't have the slightest idea he'd left a note. I'd been so upset with him for leaving with not so much as saying goodbye or texting that I'd grown angrier at myself for trusting again.

"I didn't know that," I whispered, staring at him. I shut my eyes and rested my forehead against his.

I shivered. I hadn't felt cold, but the vehicle door had been open for quite some time, and we'd let out all the heat from the truck.

"We should get you inside where it's warm," Jaxson said.

I gave in, offering my hand for him to help me out of the truck.

My boots sunk in the fresh snow as I followed him wordlessly inside his house.

He shut off the alarm as we entered, and while I wanted to continue our festivities, Skylar rushed over to greet us.

"Are you okay? I heard on the news about the hostage takeover. Do you know what they wanted? Were you there? I heard Eagle Tactical was brought in," Skylar rambled on.

I couldn't deal with her. I glanced at Jaxson and pointed at the stairwell. "I'm going to take a shower." I needed to rid myself of the filth that covered my body.

I wanted him to join me. I hoped he'd sneak away from Skylar and find his way into the bathroom with me. Unlike the last time, when he'd rescued me from the cold water crashing down against me, this time, I wanted it to be different. I needed it to be different.

One look, that was all I could give him to convey what I desired. I had to watch every word spoken with Skylar in the room and Izzie nearby.

I didn't know where she was and couldn't risk her repeating something sultry that would slip out past my lips.

I sauntered to the stairs and glanced over my shoulder, giving him the best come hither look that I could muster, and nodded toward upstairs.

I wasn't used to giving off a sexy vibe.

Would he get the hint?

CHAPTER SEVENTEEN

JAXSON

Had Ariella just shot me a sultry glance to come join her in the shower?

Was I reading into her sad gaze because I wanted her to desire me as much as I craved her?

Skylar droned on with question after question, asking about the hostage ordeal. If anyone was hurt, what they wanted, why they'd taken hostages, if there were demands, the list continued on.

I hadn't stuck around to find out why the gunmen had taken hostages. It had been obvious they were after something.

My guess was money, but they weren't about to get a truckload of cash from their heist. SWAT was handling rescuing the other hostages.

I'd been told to go home and that our services were no longer wanted after the stunt I'd pulled to save Ariella and Hazel.

It wasn't good for our company, but the local sheriff didn't seem nearly as perturbed as the lead on the case. We hadn't tried to step on any toes or insult the big guys with badges, but we did what needed to be done to save our people, and I told them I'd have done it all over again.

That's what got my ass in trouble. I had no regrets, at least not with how it went down.

My only regret was that I'd hurt Ariella.

She'd be even more upset with me if I didn't join her in the shower, assuming that was her intent.

Maybe she wanted me to sneak upstairs so we could finish what we'd started? Or I could have been completely off, and she'd reem me the minute I invited myself into the shower unannounced.

Yeah, talk about sexual harassment in the workplace. That's one for the books, but let's face it, she was living with me, her boss.

We were bound to cross some lines a little more than others.

I wanted to cross the line that with her, the one that kept us strictly as friends and professionals. I was over being just her boss.

If she gave her consent, what was the harm in falling into bed again?

Skylar continued droning on about how worried she was, how every local station had the crisis on television, and that she didn't want Izzie to see it but that she felt it necessary to watch it herself.

I found myself nodding, agreeing with her, pretending to listen, just to make the conversation over and done with.

I was being an ass, I knew, but Skylar and I didn't get along. We hadn't in years, since Dad died. She blamed me. I blamed myself. It was a great situation, really.

"Do you smell that?" I asked and sniffed my shirt. "I need to get showered and cleaned up. I stink, and I'm sure no one wants to smell this body."

Anything to get her to leave me alone for twenty minutes, maybe an hour.

"We need to talk, Jaxson, when you're done." Skylar folded her arms across her chest.

I stripped out of my shoes and headed for the stairs. "Just say it." Skylar never beat around the bush. She was brazen, a little too much so at times. Since when did she wait for permission for anything?

"I'm staying in Breckenridge permanently. I applied for a job and got hired at the coffee shop in town," Skylar said.

"Great," I muttered, storming up the stairs.

"I thought you'd be happy that I was around more," Skylar said.

"I said great!" I shouted back down at her as I hurried upstairs. The guest bathroom light was off and the door open.

Sneaky.

She'd snuck into my private bathroom. I slipped into my bedroom and noticed the bathroom light was on and the door had been left ajar.

I stripped out my clothes, my shirt on the ground, my pants, my boxers, and lastly, my socks. I opened the bathroom door naked, hoping I hadn't misread her signal.

Did she want this?

Did she want me?

I yanked back the curtain and stepped into the shower with her. Unlike the last time, when she'd been curled up on the floor, this time, she was exactly as I would have imagined, standing under the spray dripping wet.

I climbed into the steamy shower and pulled her tight. My lips crushed hers. I needed to feel her all around me.

Frenzied, I lifted one of her legs and guided myself inside her warmth, burying inside of her.

Ariella moaned as I swiftly entered her. Her fingernails gripped my back, digging in, marking me.

Her head dipped back, skin flushed. Was she blushing from desire or the heat of the shower?

Steam surrounded us.

The sound of water pouring out the shower, I prayed hid the noises we made from listening ears.

"Harder," she grunted into my ear, her teeth tugging on the lobe.

I groaned and tried to concentrate on satisfying her and not ruining an incredible moment.

I lifted her hips, her legs wrapped around me as I backed her up against the shower wall. She shivered, with her back to the interior.

"God, that's cold," she muttered and pulled me tighter, deeper, squeezing down.

It took every amount of measurable self-control I had not to disappoint her. "Won't happen again."

"I hope it does." Her breath tickled my neck before I captured her lips again.

I tried to go slow, drag out the inevitable moment, but the thought of losing her had torn me apart inside. I'd broken every protocol today. None of it mattered, only that we were here now, together.

My pace frenzied, driving deeper inside of her, needing to become one with her.

Her insides tightened, and I felt her tremble against me.

It was all the encouragement I needed. All fury unleashed as I grunted, clinging tight against her body, drinking in everything about this moment from her sweet, sexy scent down to the soft noises she made as we came undone together.

I didn't want to forget any of it, ever.

I shut off the water and carried her to my bed, laying her down, crawling above her, staring down at her.

"You're all mine, Freckles." I wanted to claim her and mark her as mine forever. While I knew she was alive and well and safe in my arms, I had to keep telling myself that she was here with me and this was real.

Her thumb stroked my jaw, and I leaned down, brushing my lips against hers, crushing her with a bruising kiss. I'd never felt quite so helpless until today, hearing about the hostage situation and that she was inside because I'd sent her there.

Guilt weighed heavily over me.

I pulled back, my elbows propped up so I could stare down at her as I settled my hips over hers, pressing her down into the mattress, covering her with my body, shielding her from the outside world, protecting her.

Her bottom lip curled between her teeth. "What's wrong?" I whispered, refusing to glance away.

She had my undivided attention. I slid my thumb over her lip, her jaw relaxed as she released her hold over the sensitive skin. Had she even realized what she'd been doing?

"You're my boss." She stared up at me, unmoving. With one hand, she caressed the stubble on my jaw, and the other rested on my lower back. "Just a few days ago, you were pretty clear sex was off-limits, that we couldn't do this and work together."

I rolled off her body and lay on my back, staring up at the ceiling with a huff. "I can't work with you and pretend you mean nothing to me."

Ariella rolled onto her side, tugging the covers up around her waist. She chewed her bottom lip again.

I leaned in, needing another taste, wanting to know she didn't regret what we'd just done. I couldn't go back to pretending that we were nothing more than friends.

Having her at the office had been driving me crazy. I'd wanted to bend her over my desk.

This kiss was softer, fueled with longing and want, not solely need and pent-up desires.

"What does that mean?" Ariella asked. "I'd rather give up my job than give up you."

My hold on her tightened. The guys would inevitably kill me, but I wouldn't let her leave the business or leave me, and being professional had been too damned hard.

"You're not leaving the team. You're one of us now." She'd proven herself, especially today, protecting Hazel, keeping her out of the hands of the men who wanted her dead.

"What are you suggesting?" she asked, staring down at me. Her fingers tapped against my chest.

I pulled the covers up around us, burying her between me and the warmth of the blankets. I kissed her cheek, nose, and eyelids, teasing her. I didn't have a great suggestion. While I wanted to shout out to the world that she was mine, I had a feeling that was too much for her. I didn't want to push her away.

"We go slow, keep what's happening between us," I said. It wasn't anyone else's business.

"Do you really think you're capable of keeping this a secret?"

I'd kept a lot of secrets. It was part of the job. I knew Ariella could handle it because she'd been required to do the same with the C.I.A.. "Yes. Why? Are you having doubts?"

Her eyes shone with mirth, and she giggled as she maneuvered her hips over mine. Her hand slipped down between the sheets, waking me up inside, making me feel alive all over again. "Oh, I can handle it, but I'm not sure grumpy bosshole will be able to pull it off," Ariella said.

I snorted. "Is that a challenge, Freckles?" She made me feel like a teenager all over again, my body instantly responding to her touch.

I was under her control and at her mercy.

———————

After staying up nearly all night satisfying each other, dawn broke. Ariella had just fallen to sleep, and I had to get up for work.

I didn't have the heart to wake her. I kissed her but also thought better of leaving a note. The last time everything had gone terribly wrong for us, and while I didn't think my house was about to burn down, I didn't need to chance some great catastrophe, either.

I kissed her softly on her cheek.

She stirred, eyes still closed, and reached out with her arm against the mattress searching for me. I stood dressed and ready to go.

"Sleep in. I'll swing by with lunch and bring you into the office around noon. Just this once, you can come in late, boss' orders."

Her eyes lazily opened. "Are you sure? I don't want special treatment."

"Really?" I stared down at her with a grin and leaned in, kissing her again. "That's not what you were moaning last night."

Her eyes lazily shut, but the smile never left her lips. She moaned softly. "Yeah, you're right. Just don't tell the guys, remember?"

"You have my word." I would keep our little secret between us, at least until I knew the guys wouldn't give Ariella a hard time.

I could handle them harassing me. What I didn't want was them pressuring me to end the relationship or to dismiss her from the job.

I planted one last kiss on her forehead before I quietly snuck out of the bedroom and shut the door. I hurried down to the kitchen, needing a strong cup of coffee to keep me awake.

"Morning," Skylar said. She sat at the kitchen table reading the newspaper.

I strode across the kitchen, grabbed a mug, and poured a steaming hot cup of coffee. Already, I could smell the pleasant aroma and wanted to taste it.

I craved that first cup to wake me up. The last thing I wanted was to drive off the road on my way to work.

Izzie had slept in, which was unusual but not unheard of when she'd had a tiring day.

I hadn't spent enough time with my daughter lately, and I'd be spending more time with Skylar if she was moving to Breckenridge.

"Are you two a thing now?" Skylar asked. "I heard you guys all night squeaking the damned bed. I had to put headphones on to drown out the noise."

I lifted my mug to my lips and took a long drag of my coffee.

I attempted to hide the smile that was plastered to my face. Maybe she'd move out of my house if we kept her up with loud, obnoxious sex.

"What?" I asked, pretending like I hadn't heard her. I wiped the smile away and put the mug down on the counter.

"You two were knocking boots all night," Skylar said. It wasn't a question.

"Daddy!" Izzie squealed, stomping down the last of the steps. Her hair was a wild mess of tangles, and her pajamas were still on, but she was a bundle of cuteness.

"Morning, baby girl." I lifted her into my arms and spun her around, giving her hugs and kisses. I'd missed her so much and had depended on Skylar more than I wanted to admit.

"Knocking boobs, Daddy. I wanna knock boobs."

Skylar's face turned crimson, and she hung her head, covering her face with her hands.

"Boots," I said, correcting Izzie. "And it's not a saying we use." She was smart enough to understand that it wasn't something nice to say if I was telling her that. I didn't need to elaborate; she was, after all, only three years old.

"Come on. Let's get you dressed." I put her down on the ground, and she grabbed my hand, tugging me to follow her upstairs.

I did my best to keep quiet, not wanting to wake Ariella.

Following Izzie to her bedroom, I flipped on the light and strode to the dresser in a hurry. I needed to get into the office and find out what was going on with Mason and Hazel.

Were they all right?

I was supposed to meet with Franco yesterday, but after he'd been held up at the resort, I suspected he might stop by today. We needed to drop them as a client. There was no way we would turn Hazel over, and while I'd been doing my due diligence on Franco, I hadn't expected to come up against the mafia.

We'd dealt with criminals in the past, domestic violence cases and delinquents, but the mafia, that was new. I wanted to discuss how we were going to handle it with the guys before Franco or his goons showed up at Eagle Tactical. We needed a plan. Telling them we weren't going to accept the job didn't seem like enough.

I opened the drawers of the dresser, retrieving an outfit for Izzie. While in the process of dressing her, my cell phone rang.

I answered the call and held it to my ear using my shoulder. "Hey, I'll be in the office soon," I said, having recognized Declan's number pop up on my phone.

"Did you see the news this morning?" Declan asked.

My stomach sunk. "No. Is everything okay? Did Mason check-in?" I asked. I hadn't spoken with him about where he was taking Hazel, but I assumed it was his uncle's property in North Dakota. The team had gathered for a retreat there on quite a few occasions.

"Mason's fine, as far as I know. This is about Ariella," Declan said.

I hurried as I dressed Izzie and glanced back at the bedroom across the hall. "What about her?"

Was there another secret she hadn't divulged that I was now going to be beaten down with?

How much more could I take?

"Do you remember Benjamin Ryan?"

"Yes, he's her ex-husband," I said. I knew of him. The bastard stole my life savings.

"The D.A. dropped the charges against him, and he's been released from prison," Declan said. "Turns out there's evidence that he couldn't have been involved since the digital trail leads to a connection in another state outside of New York. There's an interview on the news asking what he plans on doing next with his life."

I swallowed the lump in my throat. Izzie was dressed, but her clothes didn't match. I'd been too busy listening to Declan to realize until after I dressed her how much she clashed.

"Do you like leaving me hanging?" I grimaced and took her hand, leading her out of her bedroom and back down the stairwell.

"He's coming back to claim his wife, Ariella Ryan."

CHAPTER EIGHTEEN

Hazel

I had kept my head down and avoided glancing at Franco during the hostage takeover. I could still feel his putrid breath when he had kissed me before throwing me into the back of his car recently.

I had no idea where Mason and I were heading. We'd already been driving for hours, and I'd fallen asleep for a while. The comfort of the vehicle and the fact I could relax had been enough to make me succumb to sleep.

I rubbed my eyelids and stirred, shifting in the truck.

It was still dark outside. I glanced at the clock in the vehicle. It was just past midnight.

"How are you holding up?" Mason asked.

"Just tired, otherwise I'm all right," I said. My fingers played with the white gold necklace, tugging on the chain, twirling it on my index finger.

"We're almost there. As soon as we head inside, I'll make us something light to eat before bed."

"I'm not very hungry." Although my stomach grumbled otherwise, I didn't think I could eat much. The last two days' events had been exhausting, and without much sleep, the thought of food wasn't appealing.

He drove down a gravel road, kicking up dirt and dust in our wake. Where the hell had he taken me? Did they have a safe house?

Mason didn't say a word, kept his attention on the road the last couple of miles until we pulled up out front of a rustic home, two stories, on a farm.

"We're not in Montana anymore, are we?" I hadn't seen any mountains, but it was dark.

"North Dakota. My uncle owns the farm and acres of land out here. He has plenty of room, but he's not very kind to strangers. It'd be best if we pretended we were a couple."

I snorted. He couldn't be serious.

He shut off the engine and unlocked the truck's door.

"You're joking. Right?" I asked and climbed out of the vehicle, following him around to the front door.

I didn't have any clothes or possessions with me, except the clothes on my back. Everything Ariella had been kind enough to buy for me was back at the resort.

His hand fell to my lower back as he escorted me up the porch steps. "I'm serious. If we want to stay here, then we need to convince him we're serious about each other."

"Great," I muttered under my breath. It wasn't that I didn't still harbor feelings for Mason, quite the opposite.

I'd practically thrown myself at him earlier, and he'd turned me down because he was concerned with what, his reputation?

I shuffled my feet as I felt the weight of his hand against my lower back. His touch was firm and possessive, and in any other circumstance, I would have gladly pretended to be his girlfriend. I didn't have the heart to do it today or the stamina to be someone else.

Exhaustion swept over me, and I stumbled as I stood on unsteady footing.

Mason's arm wrapped around my waist. "Whoa. Are you okay?" He held me close.

I nodded and rubbed my eyes. "I guess I haven't fully woken back up."

It was a lie.

I suffered when I didn't sleep, and I hadn't gotten enough rest to classify as a decent night's sleep in two days.

"We'll get you into bed soon," Mason said.

His breath against my neck sent a shiver coursing through my body. I hoped he couldn't feel my response. He held me close against him as a dog on the opposite side of the door barked profusely and heavy footsteps stomped to unlock the door.

It had taken a while, and finally, he pulled open the wooden door, the storm door still shut and locked.

"Mason?" The man had thirty years on Mason, but they looked so much alike in the eyes, the jawline, even the build. They could have almost been brothers. "What are you doing here in the middle of the night?"

He unlocked the storm door.

The stranger glared at me but let us inside.

A brown and white mixed breed dog greeted me enthusiastically, jumping, tail wagging.

"Down, Bear!" he commanded.

Bear had to be eighty pounds of pure muscle, with beautiful coloring and brown freckles on her white face. Her nose was a golden brown that matched her fur. "She's beautiful," I said as I petted her head, and she leaned against me for more pets and cuddles.

Mason embraced his uncle in a hug. I whimpered, already missing Mason's touch and hold on me. He was quick with a hug before wrapping his arm back around my hip, pulling me tight.

Was he trying to convince his uncle that we were a couple?

"Bear sure likes you," his uncle said. "She doesn't like too many people."

I found that hard to believe with her disposition, but maybe there weren't too many people who came around to his farm.

"Uncle Jeb, this is my girlfriend Hazel," Mason said. "We planned on calling, but you know how the phone signal is out here."

Uncle Jeb waved his hand dismissively. "Better not to use the phones. You know those things are constantly being monitored. No one has any privacy anymore."

He shut and locked the front door behind us. There were several deadbolts attached to the door.

"You didn't tell me you had a girlfriend," Uncle Jeb said.

Mason held me close against him. His body heat radiated off of him and onto me. I leaned into his touch and strong embrace.

"We recently reconnected," Mason said. "We knew each other back at boarding school, dated when we were kids."

Uncle Jeb's eyes brightened. "I remember Hazel. She was the best thing that ever happened to you. Kept you out of trouble."

Was that what he said to his family when he spoke about me? I rested a hand on his chest. It wasn't difficult to fall into the role of his girlfriend. I wanted to be his. "Mason was the best thing that happened to me at boarding school, too," I said.

I wasn't trying to flatter Mason or his uncle. I only spoke the truth.

Mason shucked his coat and shoes, leaving them by the entryway of the house. I did the same, following his lead. "I hope you don't mind, but we haven't eaten anything. I was hoping to whip up something in the kitchen before bed," Mason said.

"Be my guest. My house is your house, son. I'll change the sheets in the guest room while you make your lady something to eat."

We hung our coats and placed our shoes on the mat by the door. Mason latched onto my hand and tugged for me to follow him down the hall and into the kitchen.

He flipped on the light switch, bathing the kitchen in a bright daylight glow from the lightbulbs overhead.

I grimaced and shut my eyes, trying to adjust. The foyer hadn't been overly bright, but the kitchen blinded me.

Mason flipped another switch, only lighting half the kitchen. "Better?"

"Thanks." I let go of his hand and sauntered over to the counter to sit down on one of the stools. "I'm not sure how much I can eat. Sleep, that I can do." I stifled a yawn. Just speaking about sleep, made me even more tired.

"I promise I will tuck you into bed as soon as we're done eating."

I brushed a strand of hair behind my ear. Mason stared at me, making my stomach flop. Was he really going to tuck me into bed, or was he saying that for his uncle's benefit?

His Uncle Jeb hadn't followed us into the kitchen, but that didn't mean that he wasn't listening. He'd been just a room away, down the hall. I didn't know where the guest room that he'd spoken of was located in the house. I hadn't heard footsteps travel up the stairs or down the hall.

Resting my elbows on the counter and my head in my hands, I tried to stay awake.

"You're going to fall asleep in your food just like Izzie, aren't you?" Mason said, a huge grin spread across his face.

I didn't know who Izzie was or what he was referring to. "What?"

"Jaxson's daughter." He shook his head, the smile never leaving his face. "You just remind me of someone when you're sleepy."

I mumbled, incapable of answering in full sentences. I just wanted to sleep. I shut my eyes for a brief second, just to relax, when I felt a warm arm on my back and jumped in my seat.

"Relax," Mason said. He wrapped an arm around my shoulder. "I made us a sandwich. I'd like you to eat something before we climb under the covers."

I swallowed the lump in my throat. Were we actually going to share a bed? Hours earlier, I'd wanted to, but he'd turned me down. Now we were stuck pretending that we were madly in love and together.

"Come on. You need to eat something." Mason had made a sandwich for himself. He sat on the stool beside me and took a bite of his peanut butter and jelly.

I glanced at the peanut butter and banana sandwich that he'd made for me. When we were kids, it had been my favorite. He remembered. I wasn't hungry, but I lifted the bread to my lips and took a bite to appease him.

It took forever for me to finish the sandwich. Time seemed to stand still because I was tired and ready for bed. With heavy eyes, I finished the last bite and swallowed down a glass of water.

"I promise, tomorrow, I'll make us both something a little more nutritious," Mason said. He cleaned up the dishes, washing both of our plates in the sink, rinsing, and then drying each item.

I stood, wobbling from lack of sleep. "I can help dry the dishes," I offered. I walked around the counter to the sink and grabbed a dishrag, drying the plates after he washed each one.

"Thanks," Mason said. "As soon as we're done, I'll take you upstairs and tuck you into bed."

I licked my lips. Was he planning on sharing a bed with me? I wasn't sure how traditional his uncle was, whether he'd encourage or be insulted if we stayed in the same bedroom.

"What?" he asked.

I shook my head, a tired smile on my face. "I didn't say anything."

"No, but you're thinking it."

"How do you know what I'm thinking? Since when are you a mind reader?" I asked.

He shut off the water as I dried the last plate and placed it on the drying rack. I didn't know where anything went to put the dishes away.

Mason took the dishrag, folded it, and then grabbed my hand and led me up the stairwell. Wordlessly, I followed him, willing to sleep wherever he put me.

We reached the top of the stairs, and he opened the second door on the right and flipped on the light, leading me inside.

A single queen-sized mattress was pressed up against the wall. A quilt was pulled back, and several pillows had been fluffed and positioned for guests.

"Where are you sleeping?" I asked.

He shut the bedroom door. "With you, of course," Mason said. He pulled his t-shirt over his head and then undid his belt buckle, pulling his belt free.

I stood there, frozen, watching him undress.

Were we really sharing a bed together? We'd slept beside one another dozens of nights, snuck into each other's dorms and risked expulsion, but the number of times we'd actually had sex, I could count on one hand.

He opened the dresser and tossed me a t-shirt. "You can wear this to bed if you want. It's mine. I left a few things here in case I pay Uncle Jeb a visit."

"Do you bring all your girlfriends here?" I asked. I hadn't intended to come across as jealous, but the way Mason had insisted his uncle wouldn't trust me unless we were together, I found it unsettling. "Turn around," I said.

"What?"

"I'm not undressing in front of you. Turn around."

Mason rolled his eyes and then turned around to face the door.

I quickly stripped out of my clothes, which happened to be Mason's sweats that I'd worn earlier so as not to attract attention to myself. I slipped into his t-shirt and left my panties on before crawling under the blankets.

"Okay, you can turn around," I said. He removed his jeans and folded his clothes, leaving his things on the dresser before shutting off the light and stalking to the bed in only a pair of boxers.

Did the room get warmer?

"You didn't answer my question," I said. My eyes never left his body. He looked hot half-naked, and he was incredibly good-looking with his clothes on. It was any wonder a woman hadn't already snatched him up.

"About the girlfriends? You're the only person I've brought here who's not one of my military buddies, the Eagle Tactical guys."

Mason climbed beneath the covers, leaving me plenty of space on my side of the bed.

He was a professional. Even while sharing a bed and pretending to be together, he was keeping his hands to himself.

I groaned and rolled around, restless in bed.

"What's wrong?" Mason's soft voice, I found incredibly soothing.

His hand reached out, grazing my breast before settling on my side. Had it been an accident in the darkness, or had he wanted to touch me intimately?

"Aside from the fact I'm exhausted?"

"Fair enough. Get some sleep," he said. His lips grazed my cheek and planted a soft, gentle kiss against my skin.

"You don't have to pretend in here. It's just you and me."

His uncle couldn't see us in the privacy of the bedroom. He didn't have to pretend that he wanted to be with me. He'd already rejected me once today. I wasn't going to throw myself at him again.

"I would never pretend. I mean outside of Uncle Jeb, but that's just because he's paranoid about the government and what I do for a living."

Sighing, I curled up on my side, my eyes shut. I wasn't sure how much longer I'd last awake. "He's not wrong. I mean about what you do, the danger that follows you around."

I was part of that danger, risking his life, calling him for help to deal with Franco.

Would I ever be able to live my life again in a normal way, or would I be forced to go into hiding or witness protection?

"I can defend myself," Mason said. "Besides, nothing is going to happen to you while I'm with you."

He was so confident in his answer. I found comfort in his words. I shifted on the bed, inching closer. While I didn't reach out to touch him, I brushed against him, and knowing he was next to me made me at ease.

"You trust Uncle Jeb?"

"With my life," Mason said. "He won't let anything happen to you, either. Get some sleep." His lips grazed my cheek once more before the bed shifted, and he pulled me into his arms, cradling me.

I opened my mouth to object, to point out this wasn't professional, but it took too much energy and stamina that I didn't have to fight with him. I let him hold me and protect me.

My legs tangled in his, pulling him closer, the heat of our bodies stirring desires that intensified within me. I couldn't have him. He wasn't mine. Not anymore.

———

I awoke with a start. Bear was barking profusely downstairs. My body froze, the lights were off, the sky still dark.

I didn't know what time it was, but I felt much better, more rested. I'd slept for a while.

I reached out for Mason, but he wasn't in bed with me. "Mason?" I whispered into the darkness, unable to see him.

He didn't respond. Maybe he was downstairs and he'd startled Bear?

The sound of gunfire erupted from the lower level.

CHAPTER NINETEEN

MASON

I'd been startled awake, but by what, I wasn't sure. Hazel slept soundly, curled up on her side.

I untangled from her grasp and quietly grabbed my gun on the dresser tucked beneath my pants.

I headed out of the bedroom, and Uncle Jeb was in the hallway, shotgun in hand.

His eyes, tight and narrow, focused on the same thing I was, listening for what had awoken both of us.

My uncle had served in the marines many years ago. I gave him hand signals, not wanting to make a sound.

Bear howled from down below, and I hurried, gun drawn as I tore down the stairs as quietly as possible.

I needed to protect Hazel, and the best way to do that was to keep her upstairs and out of harm's way.

Uncle Jeb followed just behind me with his shotgun.

I didn't want to tell him he'd need more firepower than that if the men who were after Hazel had shown up. How had they found her? I'd been careful, making sure that no one had tailed my truck.

Had there been a tracker on the vehicle or on Hazel?

I'd given her the bangle, but there was no way that they could have hacked into our tracker. I was confident in our equipment and the security measures that we'd taken to ensure her safety.

Bear growled and barked. The sweet dog had been trained to attack. She'd sensed danger as much as we had.

Uncle Jeb came up on my right side while I flanked left and headed down the hallway. We left the lights off, to our advantage. My uncle knew his house in the dark, and I'd spent enough summers visiting that I was familiar with the layout.

Gunfire erupted from all angles outside, firing into the farmhouse. I hit the ground for cover. There was nowhere else to go. I crawled on my stomach toward the window. When the firing ceased after several long rounds, I poked my head up to see what awaited us.

There were dozens of vehicles with their lights on and engines running just outside the house.

I needed more manpower.

Even if I gave Hazel a weapon, it wouldn't be enough. I hurried back up the stairs and threw the door open.

She stood in the middle of the bedroom, pulling on the sweatshirt, getting dressed. I grabbed her arm and dragged her to come with me. "We need to get you out of here. It's a bloodbath."

I wouldn't wait for them to come and take her.

Uncle Jeb shot off his weapon. With every shot, he had to reload, costing us precious time.

Bullets tore through the house, ripping apart the walls. The men outside didn't have shotguns or pistols. They had semi-automatic weapons and didn't have to reload as often.

The first round had burned through the first floor. After they reloaded, they were now aiming haphazardly upstairs, wrecking every inch of the property that they could, ensuring there were no survivors.

I sheltered Hazel, covered her with my body as I lay above her on the floor. Fragments of wood and glass sliced my skin.

My arms burned, and blood dripped from my cheek. I ignored the pain. All that mattered was getting her out of here alive.

The firing ceased, and I grabbed Hazel by the arm, hoisting her to her feet. She trembled in my grip.

"We need to move." I led her down the stairs, my hand in hers, as I pulled her with me and kept her close to my body.

The headlights from the vehicles outside shined inside the farmhouse through the bullet holes.

Uncle Jeb sat on the floor, slumped down. Blood trickled from his chest and neck as he gasped for breath. "Get her... out of here."

"Everyone inside! Sweep the place. I want her dead or alive," Franco shouted his orders to the men outside.

I dragged Hazel with me down to the laundry room. Beneath the floor, was a false door. I pulled the board and opened the hatch. "Get in."

She shook her head violently and folded her arms across her chest. She'd been trembling earlier, but now she was shaking even more wildly.

I ran a hand over her cheek. I hadn't seen any blood on her, except for a few cuts and scrapes from the bullet shrapnel.

"I can't."

"You have to." We were running out of time. I needed her to hide, and then I had to cover the trap door to protect her. I didn't have time to even consider how I'd handle the men as they charged inside the house.

"I'm claustrophobic," she said.

"Shit. Then you're going to have to run." I prayed the men were all coming in through the front and back entrance. I hurried toward the side of the house, away from the doors, and used my elbow to clear the fragments of glass that were not fully broken and fell in the firefight.

I didn't see any men, but I could hear them. I helped Hazel through the window along with Bear, hoping that she'd protect Hazel.

Men came stampeding through the house, guns drawn. I hurried out of the room, not wanting to give Hazel's whereabouts to any of the men searching for her.

A thick Russian accent permeated the room. "Where is she?"

Uncle Jeb coughed and wheezed. I could hear his struggle.

I skirted the corner of the room and hugged the wall, peeking out to see one man towering over my uncle.

Another man shoved his foot onto my uncle's chest, making it harder for him to breathe.

I lifted the barrel of my gun and fired several shots, hitting the men before I took off through the darkened house, hiding from them in the dining room.

Bullets blasted through the farmhouse, tearing into my arm and burning me like lava, scorching my flesh. I winced and bit my tongue to keep my groaning at bay. No one could know where I hid.

It wasn't my first bullet wound, but it didn't sting any less. Blood dripped down my arm, making it harder for me to use two hands to aim, and the bastard had shot my good arm.

"We've got her!" a voice echoed from outside.

I stumbled forward. Why hadn't she fought back? I didn't hear so much as a scream pass her lips.

Heavy boots retreated through the house, but not before sending off one last wave of bullets. I dove for cover. A second round slammed into my chest, knocking me to the floor, unable to move.

I tried to stand, to lift myself up from the ground and fight. Inch by inch, I dragged myself across the dining room floor and then into the hallway.

A streak of blood followed me across the wood flooring. I wouldn't let Hazel be dragged off with Franco.

Car doors slammed, and headlights faded as the sound of tires squealed, and vehicles tore away from the farmhouse.

She was gone, and I was to blame.

I hadn't been able to save her or protect her.

CHAPTER TWENTY

Hazel

I slipped out through the broken window.

Glass tore at my feet. My shoes were by the front door, and I had no way of getting them before fleeing the farmhouse.

I ran hard and fast, with Bear at my side, in the darkness outside through the field. Breathing hard, I stumbled over a rock, smashing my toe and landing face-first against the ground.

Dirt covered my face and filled my mouth. I spit and coughed.

Gunfire erupted from behind me inside the house. Bear took off, abandoning me in the open field.

"Mason," I whispered, staring at the battered farmhouse. It hadn't fallen yet. The structure looked unstable from the hundreds of bullet holes that littered the walls.

I needed to run, but my feet were sore and raw. My heart wanted to save Mason, but the only way to do that was to surrender to Franco. Even that didn't secure Mason's freedom.

A flashlight shined right on me.

"Freeze! Hold it right there!" a gruff voice shouted at me.

I ran, hoping the darkness would blanket me, but there was a full moon.

He shot off a warning. The bullet whizzed by my side.

"Stop! Next time, I won't miss."

I came to an abrupt halt, my arms in the air. "Don't shoot. I'll go with you. Just leave my friends alone." It wasn't a bargain I could make. I had no leverage. He had the gun on me, but I still said it anyhow.

He snorted, grabbed my arm and yanked me to follow before he let go and rammed the gun into my back.

"Move faster," he commanded. As we drew closer, he shouted at the others. "We got her!"

I glanced down at the golden bangle hidden on my arm beneath the sweatshirt. Mason would find me, assuming he was still alive.

I couldn't allow myself to think like that. He was a fighter, always had been, even at boarding school.

The men repeatedly fired on the farmhouse, another round of bullets showering the building and the two men inside.

Uncle Jeb hadn't looked in good shape when I'd come downstairs. We should have checked on him, helped him, put him into the hidden crawl space under the house.

My stomach ached, wretched with guilt.

Had I just married Franco, none of this would have happened.

"There's my little firecracker," Franco said as he stomped through the grass, coming right for me.

I wanted to flee, but I couldn't move. The gun was nestled against my spine. My feet throbbed, which made it difficult to walk.

He fisted my hair and tugged on the strands, jerking my head up and my gaze, to meet his stern expression. "No more running, Hazel. The chase is over."

He dragged me by the hair and shoved me into the back of his town car, sliding in beside me.

"Don't even try escaping. Child locks are an incredible feature." His knees were spread wide, taking up a seat and a half.

I scooted as close as I could to the opposite door, trying to make myself small.

"It's a shame you killed those men and the marshals," Franco said. "I never thought my wife would take part in the messy aspects of the business, but it seems you're as dirty as I am."

"I didn't kill anyone."

I wasn't the murderer.

He couldn't blame me for what he did.

Franco turned to face me. "You don't believe that. I know the way you think. You're more guilty than I am. You reached out to him and sealed his fate."

His finger grazed my collarbone and touched the white gold chain my father had given me, holding a heart locket with a picture of my deceased mother.

He ripped the necklace from my neck, rolled down the window, and tossed it outside as we drove.

"No!" I gasped, feeling both naked and broken without the chain. I hadn't taken it off in years. It had become a part of me. "Why?" my voice croaked. "That was from my father!" Tears threatened my vision. I hadn't cried with all that I'd experienced, but now stealing a piece of me and disposing of it like trash. I couldn't take much more.

"I know. How do you think I was able to find you?" he asked.

I didn't understand, frowning as he stared at me. I shook my head. Was he going to elaborate?

Franco stretched his arm and wrapped it around my shoulders. I swallowed the lump in my throat as he pulled me tight against him and his lips grazed my ear. "Your father wanted to make sure you were safe.

How do you think I was able to find you?" he whispered.

I shivered and pulled away, untangling from his grasp. "There was a tracker in the necklace? Let me go."

I didn't want to believe it, but how else had Franco been able to find me? Mason hadn't called anyone when we'd left Breckenridge. We'd shown up unannounced in North Dakota on his uncle's farm.

"I'm never letting you go," Franco whispered into my ear.

The hair on my arms stood on end.

I shimmied away, but his grip on my shoulders tightened.

————

We drove through the night straight to Chicago. I kept as far from Franco as possible in the back of the car. After some time, his hand fell away from my shoulder, and I'd been able to relax and fall asleep in short bursts.

The vehicle came to a standstill, and I stirred awake.

Rubbing the sleep from my eyes, I recognized the gated house. It had been my father's home before he'd died and left it to Nikolai.

"What are we doing here?" I asked.

Franco didn't answer me.

The driver opened the window, punched in a code, and proceeded forward to the front entrance before he shut off the engine and stepped out.

He opened the door for Franco.

Franco climbed out of the car and reached in, grabbed my arm, he dragged me out with him.

"Get off me." I attempted to shrug out of his grasp, but he didn't let me free.

There was nowhere to run, even if I could manage to escape. The wrought-iron fence had arrows at the top, ensuring no one would climb in or out. Not to mention my feet were swollen and gashed from the glass I'd stepped on last night in my plight for freedom.

Victor, one of my father's oldest friends, stepped out through the front door and down the stairs. He had thinning white hair and was scrawny compared to Franco. "Nikolai isn't here," Victor said.

"Fine. We'll wait." Franco released his hold on me, and I pulled farther away to keep out of his grasp.

I rubbed my bruised arms and stepped off the cement to let my sore feet sink into the grass. I didn't care that it was winter. The cold breeze made me numb, helping relieve the pain that I felt all over my body, the burning sting against my raw skin.

"It could be a while until he's back. Nikolai went to Breckenridge when he couldn't get ahold of you," Victor said.

My arms nestled tight across my chest as I shivered and glanced back at the car. At least the shelter of the vehicle and the seat had provided comfort.

Was there any chance that the driver had left the keys unattended, and I could steal the car and flee?

It was wishful thinking.

"Come inside," Victor said. "I'll call Nikolai and let him know you both have arrived."

The driver climbed back into the vehicle and started the engine, leaving me to follow Franco and Victor inside. I still didn't know why we'd come, but I suspected Nikolai wouldn't be pleased to see me.

Dried blood coated my body, and under the morning light, there were bloodstains on my arms, hands, and feet.

I limped up the wooden stairs and into the foyer.

Franco leaned in and sniffed my neck.

I shuddered and winced, disgusted.

"Find yourself a bathroom. No wife of mine will look this filthy," he said and yanked me by the hips. He pulled me close and tight against his body. "Freshen up for me. I like a girl who smells good."

I wanted to puke.

"I'll call Nikolai. Franco, please have a seat. Make yourself at home," Victor said.

Relieved when Franco released his hold on me, I hurried out of his clutches and up the stairs. The pain tore at my feet, but I kept a quickened pace. I wanted to get away, and I wasn't capable of running with tiny shards of glass still embedded in the soles of my feet.

The house smelled musty and old. While the interior hadn't changed much since Nikolai took possession of the property, the stench wreaked of his filth.

How many men had he murdered inside his home?

I hobbled to my childhood bedroom and ripped open the door. I stumbled inside, my feet leaving a trail of fresh blood on the perfectly white carpet.

I ignored the stains and the mess as I approached my closet. I'd spent many nights in the bedroom, not just in my childhood years.

I retrieved a sweater dress and black leggings from the dresser, along with undergarments.

I hurried into the nearest bathroom. There were no locks on the doors, no real privacy, just a semblance of it. I'd have to trust that no one would invade my personal space. There was no furniture to slide in front of the door.

As a kid living in the giant house, it hadn't mattered. No one had barreled through the bathroom door, but now, knowing that Franco could force his way in on a whim, my stomach ached.

I stripped down and turned on the shower, letting the steam permeate the bathroom while I retrieved a pair of tweezers from the medicine cabinet.

I sat on the closed toilet lid, lifting one leg at a time to remove any glass or debris buried in the bottoms of my feet.

I breathed loudly through my mouth, exhaling and grimacing as I grabbed the splinters of wood and shards of glass that had snuck under my skin.

"One down," I said. I worked diligently on my other foot before I finally climbed under the hot spray of the shower.

Staring down at the water, the clear spray at my feet turned brown and red as I washed away the remnants of yesterday.

What didn't wash away was the pain, the concern for Mason and his uncle. I hadn't removed the bracelet, keeping it against my skin. I hoped it could get wet, but it was too late. I'd already left it on under the shower spray.

I couldn't remove it. What if Franco stormed into the bathroom and took my clothes and bracelet? We weren't staying at this home for more than a few hours, however long it took for Nikolai to return.

We had driven more than fourteen hours, but my brother had a private plane. I expected that he'd flown to Montana and then flown home.

Why had he come all the way to Breckenridge? What had he hoped to do, convince me to return with him?

My brother was the biggest asshole on the planet, with a God complex. He was also the reason I never ended up in California. My father had spent the money that was earmarked for my tuition on Nikolai. He'd also told me it was too dangerous for me to be outside of Chicago and kept me trapped, but I wasn't a prisoner, not completely.

I'd been given permission to come and go from the property. I'd believed I had freedom, but it was a sham. The necklace he'd given me had provided my whereabouts. I was never alone, even when I wanted to be.

My father had helped me land my first job straight out of high school. Most hires with only a high school diploma started out landing a gig in retail or low pay work, something entry-level and mundane.

The water washed over me, cleansing me of my sins. I opened the shampoo bottle and squeezed a dollop-sized amount into my hand before lathering my hair.

I'd never had a typical entry-level position. I had wanted to go to college for graphic design, and my father had told me to send my resume to West Marketing Firm. I'd done exactly what he asked and had been hired at my first interview as the marketing manager.

Two months later, I was promoted to marketing director when my boss mysteriously disappeared.

Looking back, it had all been suspect, the employees, the clients, they'd all been Nikolai's friends and family, business partners in some way or another. I hadn't known that when I was eighteen.

I'd been naïve and foolish into believing everything Daddy said was true.

My father had lied to me and had me believe that I held a job at a prestigious firm straight out of high school because I'd had raw talent.

I rinsed the suds from my hair and soaped every inch of my skin.

The bathroom door thrust open, and a cold gust of wind followed the intruder.

"Get out!" I shouted and pulled the curtain tight around myself, hiding both my body and my bracelet from sight.

Franco's dark laugh filled the bathroom. "No point in being shy with me. We're going to be husband and wife."

"Over my dead body," I snarled.

"That can be arranged." He stepped closer, invading my personal space, and grabbed my jaw, forcing me to stare into his dark, soulless eyes. "You've been in here long enough. Get dressed and come downstairs."

He released his hold on me.

I breathed a sigh of relief.

"You've got five minutes. Any longer, and I'll pull out the cane. You'll discover the beauty of discipline and submission."

"I'll never submit to you."

Franco backhanded me across the face.

My cheek stung, and my eyes shut from the initial shock and pain. No one had ever hit me before, certainly not my face.

"Never is a long time. We have the rest of our lives together," Franco said, reminding me that I was *his*.

His phone buzzed in his pants, and he took a step back.

I shut off the shower, gesturing for him to get out of the bathroom.

"Nikolai, yes, I've recovered your sister. She's been quite the little firecracker," Franco said into the phone and paused.

I didn't budge from my position in the bathtub, standing with the curtain around my body, waiting for him to get out of the bathroom so I could have some privacy.

"I see. Yes, that's right. Very well," he said and smiled. "I will see you in a bit." He hung up the phone and shoved it back into his pocket.

"Get out!" I pointed at the door.

His eyes narrowed as he leaned closer, his rotten breath hitting me in the face. "I don't take orders from you." He shoved his lips over mine, forcing his tongue into my mouth.

I kept my lips closed and tried to back away, but there wasn't much place for me to run to with the shower curtain attached.

He slid his hand down inside the curtain, groping my breast. "I should fully inspect the merchandise before purchase," Franco said with a crooked grin. "You've been irritating. I should make sure I'm getting exactly what I paid for."

CHAPTER TWENTY-ONE

JAXSON

"Morning," Declan said as he came into my office. He perched himself at the edge of my desk. "What are you working on?"

I hadn't so much as looked up when he'd come into the room.

I let out a heavy sigh and ran a hand through my hair. "Trying to get ahold of Mason. After the day we all had yesterday, I thought it would be a good idea to try the satellite phone."

"He didn't answer?" Declan asked, his brow tight as he stood and came around to see what I was doing on the computer.

"No, he hasn't answered. If he'd have picked up when I called, I wouldn't have been quite so concerned. I tried calling his uncle since I'm sure that's where he went, but he's not picking up, either."

"We're talking about Uncle Jeb. That's not a surprise. The man probably ripped out his phone line. You know how paranoid he is. You've met the guy."

I slid away from my desk and stood. "True."

I strode out of the office to the hallway where the coffeepot was situated. I needed a strong cup of coffee to get me through my day.

"I just have a bad feeling. Mason should have checked in with us. I'm not happy that he took Hazel and left town without saying anything to us."

Aiden stepped into the hallway, his arms crossed as he leaned against his open door, listening and weighing in on what we said. "You could call the local sheriff's office and have them do a wellness check."

"That'll go over really well, especially with Uncle Jeb," I said.

Declan poured a cup of coffee and took it over to his desk. "I can hack into surveillance footage and see if anything looks suspicious."

That would at least be a start. It wasn't something that I was capable of doing. "Thank you," I said.

Five minutes behind the computer, and Declan had hacked the satellite footage and zoomed in on the farmhouse.

"Shit," I muttered under my breath as I stood over his shoulder. The exterior was in disarray. It was difficult to tell what extent of damage the farmhouse had sustained, but the structure didn't appear stable.

"I'll get us a ride via chopper," Aiden said as he hurried back to his office and started making phone calls.

Our connections with local and state authorities often came in handy. We had a few friends who were federal, and while we usually helped them, this time, we were reaching out for their assistance.

I reached out to the county sheriff's department where Mason and Uncle Jeb were located. They were sending a team to check on the situation while we arranged transportation to the scene.

———

Before our helicopter arrived, we received a call from the county sheriff's office in North Dakota, informing us that EMTs were being called and they had found two bodies. Mason was alive, but his uncle hadn't made it.

"Mason wants to talk to you," the sheriff said. He had called using Mason's phone and put on the video feed so that we could talk.

I stepped out of the room and into my office, leaving the door open.

"It's good to see you, Mason," I said. He looked like hell, pale, blue-tinged lips, but he was conscious and breathing.

He tried to speak, but I couldn't hear him. Mason was far too quiet for the phone to pick up what he said.

"I can't hear you, buddy. It'll be okay. Go with the EMTs and let them do their job." I tried to assure him that everything was fine.

He looked like hell. He was lucky to still be alive.

The sheriff leaned down to hear what Mason was trying to say to us. "Hazel has a tracker."

I sipped my coffee. "Yes, that makes sense. It's probably how they were able to find you guys."

Mason shook his head. That wasn't the message that he was trying to convey. He gestured the sheriff close again.

The video on the phone shifted, giving a glimpse of the blood and the damage to the property. Mason had lost a significant amount of blood, but he was breathing. His heart was beating. He was a fighter.

"Hazel has a bracelet you can track. He gave it to her to protect her," the sheriff said. He frowned, glancing from Mason to me. "Who exactly are you guys?"

"Eagle Tactical," I said. I'd already told his office that when I called and requested their assistance, but either he didn't get the memo or didn't know who we were. "Mason, we'll get Hazel back. You let the EMTs and the doctors look after you. Get better, okay?"

We'd pay him a visit when Hazel was safe and out of harm's way.

I hung up the phone and hurried into the office with Declan.

"I got all of that," Declan said before I could relay the message. "I'm already on the bracelet and tracking Hazel's whereabouts. Shit." He glanced away from his computer monitor at me. "She's back in Chicago."

"Get the address. I'll call Colton Carr and see if he can get to her with a team before we can get there." I grabbed my coat and gulped the last of my coffee.

"What about Izzie?" Declan asked. "Maybe we should send Aiden and Lincoln?"

"Lincoln's busy with the insurance adjuster after what the bastards did to his restaurant," Aiden said from across the hallway. His boots clunked on the floor as he hurried into the office with us. "I'll come with you. We need at least a two-man team."

I laughed under my breath. I doubted two of us and the U.S. marshal would be enough to take down the Russian mafia in Chicago and rescue Hazel. "Declan, you stay here and track Hazel. Aiden, call Lincoln and tell him we need him ASAP. Offer him full-time, again. We need his help.

We need all the help we can get," I muttered under my breath.

Declan glanced at me. His voice was tentative. "We could call Jayden. I know it's not ideal, but we could use the manpower."

"Absolutely not." I wasn't inviting an off-gridder to our team. Jayden may have been one of us in the military, one of our unit and our team, but he'd chosen them over us. "They're responsible for the hostage takeover at the resort yesterday."

"You don't know that Jayden was part of that; everyone involved wore masks," Declan said.

"Why are you defending him?" I asked. "And not everyone involved wore a mask. Emma was there, and so was Jayden. I stripped his ass bare and stole his clothes."

"Shit. You didn't tell us that." Aiden laughed. "I would have liked to have seen that. Any chance you took a picture?"

I rolled my eyes and grabbed my truck keys on the desk. "I didn't have time. Too bad, right? I'm heading out to the hanger. I'll call Carr on the way. Are you coming, Aiden?" I asked.

"I wouldn't miss the opportunity to kick some ass. Let me call Lincoln while we're in the car."

"Shit. I need to call Ariella too. I told her I'd pick up lunch and bring her back with me to the office." That wasn't going to happen. Maybe she'd be able to get Skylar to drive her to the resort to pick up her car. If not, I'd give her a lift tomorrow or when I got home.

———

Lincoln, Aiden, and I teamed up in Chicago with Colton Carr and his team of U.S. Marshals along with the Federal Bureau of Investigation.

"She's still on the property," Declan said.

He forwarded her location to my phone.

Examining the screen on my cell phone, there was a tiny red dot that blinked as it appeared to pace back and forth.

I wasn't sure whether the position was approximate or she was in fact moving, but we had her whereabouts, as long as the bracelet was still on her.

"We've got a team ready to go," Agent Bishop said. He was dressed in a suit, his team in SWAT gear surrounding the perimeter.

We stood just outside of the command center, a vehicle set up on the side of the road around the block and out of sight.

A young woman with long blonde hair wearing a Kevlar vest stormed into the command post. "I've got eyes and ears on the place. You should be getting a signal any moment."

She sat down in front of a monitor and adjusted the frequency, picking up the video feed and audio of Hazel.

"That's her. That's our target to extract," I said, giving confirmation.

"SWAT goes in first," Agent Bishop said. He was tall and lanky. He'd probably never spent a day in the military, but he commanded with authority.

"Fine," Lincoln said. He stood behind me, arms folded across his chest. He hadn't moved an inch, not even to step out of the way as agents came and went, having to squeeze past him in the narrow hallway.

"Do we have a visual on Nikolai Agron?" I asked.

"Not yet," Agent Bishop said. "We have confirmation that Franco Ivanov is there, along with another man we're running through our database. There are also a number of support staff, but the key players for the mafia don't appear to be onsite."

"Other than Franco," I said. He was one of the key players, and while he may not have been the head of the mafia, he was second in command and the reason we were here.

Agent Bishop watched from the screen as he gave commands to his fellow agents. They entered the perimeter of the property and came up along the house. "Wait until I give all-clear to enter."

I stared at the screen from over his shoulder. They were waiting until Hazel would be out of immediate danger.

She wasn't near the foyer. It would take several seconds from the breach until they entered the room where she was located.

Enough time to shoot her or grab her as a hostage and threaten her life.

I hated watching on the screen, unable to be part of the action.

My hands bunched into fists.

Franco stepped out of the room, leaving Hazel with the unidentified man in the house.

"Now!" Agent Bishop commanded as the SWAT team broke down the front door and barreled inside, guns drawn, announcing their presence.

Gunfire erupted from every angle. I shivered and swallowed the bile rising in my throat. I was used to being in the field, not watching from a monitor. It was painful knowing there was nothing I could do to help.

I wanted to go outside, be part of the action, but that wasn't an option. Agent Bishop had made it clear that we were allowed in the command post as a courtesy of Colton Carr.

I paced the small length of the trailer, finding it impossible to stand still while I kept my gaze on the monitors and surveillance footage from around the property.

One camera lost visual footage, but the audio was still patched in, which felt almost worse with the sound of gunfire and gut-wrenching screams.

I pinched the bridge of my nose, pushing down memories of my time overseas in the military. The horrors were resurfacing at the sounds of men screaming.

There wasn't more I could do, and so I waited with Aiden and Lincoln. SWAT apprehended Franco as well as several other individuals in the household before bringing Hazel outside.

I hurried out of the command post, with Lincoln and Aiden on my heels.

Her eyes were puffy and red, her cheeks flushed. She tore outside, hobbling away from the armed agents when she saw us. Her brow furrowed, and tears welled in her eyes. "Mason," she whispered.

A single word, and I understood all the fears that were likely flooding through her. "We got to him in time. He's at the hospital," I said.

We had called and checked on him the moment we arrived in Chicago to make sure that he hadn't declined.

"He's stable," I said, hoping that would ease her mind.

She exhaled a heavy sigh. "Thank you."

Agent Bishop came up from behind. "We have a few questions for Hazel," he said.

"Sure. I'll answer anything I can." Hazel wrapped her arms around her chest.

Aiden grabbed an emergency blanket from the command post and pulled it over Hazel's shoulders.

"Thanks," she said.

Agent Bishop nodded his appreciation to Aiden before returning his attention to Hazel. "Do you know where your brother Nikolai is right now? We know this is his property."

"We were waiting for him to fly home. He was in Breckenridge looking for me." She exhaled a heavy breath and stared at the ground. "He should have returned home by now."

I spun around on my heels, noting the road had been closed off. He'd probably been on his way home and saw our agents. "He didn't call or reach out to Franco while you were in the house?" I asked.

Hazel shook her head. "Franco was focused on me." She swiped the tears as quickly as they'd fallen down her cheek. "Victor had been the one to call him, not Franco, but they did talk on the phone. I don't know what was said, I was in the shower at the time. Can we be done? I want to go see Mason."

Agent Bishop jotted down the little information that Hazel was able to provide. "Yes, of course. I believe we should be putting you into protective custody. With your brother out there and running the mafia, it's only a matter of time until he finds you."

"She'll stay in our protective custody," I said. Hazel had reached out to us, and without a doubt, it was what Mason would want for her.

"Are you sure that's what you want, Hazel?" Agent Bishop asked. "We have a safe house that we can transport you to, provide you with a new identity, and ensure your safety."

She lifted her gaze and met Agent Bishop's hardened expression. "As much as I appreciate your offer, the U.S. Marshals weren't able to protect me. I doubt you can, either. I'll take my chances with Eagle Tactical. Besides, I want to see Mason."

"You do realize that is probably where Nikolai is heading, to the one person he knows you want to be with," Agent Bishop said.

"You have the contact information for Eagle Tactical. If you need anything from me, you can reach out to them until I replace my cell phone," Hazel said.

"Very well," Agent Bishop said before he headed back to the command post, their operation complete.

Lincoln stepped closer to Hazel, lifting her chin. "We'll bring you to Mason if that's what you want, but your brother is still out there. Agent Bishop is right; we're leading you right into danger if we take you to him. You need to be aware of the risks."

My phone vibrated in my pocket. I reached into my jacket and grabbed my phone, glancing at the caller ID, recognizing Ariella's phone number. "Hey, we're just finishing up here in Chicago," I said, answering the phone.

"Jaxson. You need to come home." Ariella didn't sound like herself.

"What's wrong? Is Izzie all right?"

"It's Nikolai. He's here and—"

The phone went dead.

CHAPTER TWENTY-TWO

ARIELLA

"Izzie, do we have to play hide and seek again?" I asked, exasperated.

I adored Jaxson's daughter, but she was a constant bundle of energy, and she'd already hidden a dozen times. She didn't grasp taking turns, and she liked to hide in the same place every time.

The doorbell interrupted our game.

I headed to the front door and attempted to glance through the peephole, but it was too tall for me. It had clearly been drilled for Jaxson.

Pulling the door open, Emma stood on the opposite side trembling, covered in blood. Her hair was wet, her clothes muddy and torn.

Rain pelted outside, the weather a few degrees above freezing.

"Come inside," I said, ushering her into the house and disabling the alarm. Jaxson had given me a secondary code that I was to use while he was away.

Her teeth chattered, and she rubbed her arms in an attempt to warm up.

"What happened?" I locked the door behind her and armed the alarm. She looked like she could have been mauled by a bear.

I glanced her over from head to toe. Maybe it wasn't that bad. She still had her arms and legs, but she looked in bad shape.

"I was at my place and he started shooting."

"Who started shooting?" I pulled out my phone. "We need to call the police."

Her eyes were wide and frantic. "No police."

She put a hand on my phone, her wet fingers making a mess of my device. I wiped it down and shoved it back into my pocket for the moment.

"If someone broke into your house and started shooting people, we need to call the sheriff," I said.

"Ella?" Izzie said, attempting to say my name. It was cute and amusing, considering she could say 'Ariel' and 'Ella' but refused to put them together. Honestly, I didn't mind the nickname. It was endearing.

I picked Izzie up, holding her in my arms, protecting her from Emma.

Emma didn't look well, and the fact she wasn't letting me call for help had me worried she wasn't herself.

Emma stared at Isabella, transfixed by the little girl, her biological daughter.

When was the last time she'd seen her? Had it been when she'd dropped her off and left her with Jaxson?

I'd heard the story from Jaxson about how Emma had intended to give her up and asked him to sign away his parental rights, but I'd never heard her speak of it, ever.

The long, sad stare at Izzie had my stomach in knots. I gently put Izzie down on the sofa and grabbed Emma by the arm and dragged her into the kitchen. "What the hell is going on?" I asked. I stood so that Emma's back was to Izzie and I could keep an eye on the little girl.

"He came and killed everyone." Emma's normally porcelain skin was sickeningly pale. Sweat glistened her forehead.

I reached for a clean rag and dampened it in the sink, adding a touch of soap and suds, helping clean her abrasions on her forehead. She needed a shower, though, and a fresh change of clothes.

"Who came?" I asked, trying to get it out of her. I wanted to know what happened.

Was it the men who had been after Hazel? Why would they have gone to Emma's home? The two women didn't look anything alike. She shouldn't have been mistaken for Hazel.

"I fucked up, royally." Emma swiped at her nose. Her eyes were red and brimmed with tears.

I reached for her hand, giving it a reassuring squeeze. "Whatever you did, I'm sure it can be fixed."

"I don't think so. They're dead because of me."

While I didn't know Emma that well, I didn't believe she had it in her to kill anyone. We'd worked together for a short time at the resort and been friends. Although, lately, we hadn't seen much of one another, I couldn't believe she had done anything that terrible. She had to be overreacting, right?

"Who is dead?" I needed to get her to open up and confide in me.

She wiped the tears and I grabbed a paper towel, offering it to her to dry her eyes.

"Thanks," she said between sniffles. "All of them. At least, I think they all are. I ran out the back door while they shot up the compound."

I didn't understand what she was talking about. "The compound? Don't you live in one of the cabins near the resort?"

"I only had that place while I was interviewing for the job. I've been living with the guys up there," Emma said and gestured north on the mountain.

My voice caught in my throat. "The off-gridders?" Jaxson had warned me to steer clear of them and the entrance to their compound.

Emma dabbed at her eyes with the paper towel.

I pulled out my cell phone and dialed the local police, letting him know who I was, that I worked for Eagle Tactical, and what Emma had witnessed. If what Emma said was true, they needed a team to scout the compound for survivors.

Jaxson would have been called in along with the rest of the Eagle Tactical team if they'd have been in town. I'd call him later when things settled down for a bit. There was no reason to worry him. He was busy en route to Chicago.

———

The sheriff's department paid us a visit after checking out the compound. "Emma, I need to bring you in for your formal statement."

Emma reached for my hand. "Will you come with me?"

"Sure. Let me bundle Izzie up, and then we can follow you down to the station," I said. I couldn't say no. She was broken. I knew what that felt like, to have your world crumble apart all around you.

I grabbed a snack from the vending machine at the police station for Izzie while we went into a separate room. "Come with me." The sheriff opened the door to an adjoining room and flipped on the lights. "You'll be able to see and hear everything. Make yourself comfortable. Hopefully, this won't take long."

Did he usually let people watch when statements were given?

Had he given me special treatment because he knew that I worked for Eagle Tactical?

I let Izzie sit on a table with her back to the glass window as I watched through the one-way mirror.

The sheriff stepped into the room with Emma and shut the door. "Can I get you something to drink? Coffee? Water?"

"No, thank you." Emma sat with her hands on the metal table. She looked incredibly calm after all that had transpired, but she was probably just in shock. Right?

He retrieved a pad of paper and pen. "Can you tell me what happened today?"

Emma exhaled a heavy sigh. "Yes." She glanced from the table to the sheriff. "I was at home, at the compound, when two men came in with guns drawn and began shooting everyone in sight."

"Do you know either of these men?" the sheriff asked.

"I've never seen them before."

"Are you sure? Can you recall if you saw them at the resort?"

She shook her head. "No. I never saw them at the resort or anywhere before. They weren't locals."

He exhaled heavily out of his nostrils. "Interesting. Can you tell me anything else? Like what might have made two men, who have never been to the resort or possibly even this town, come up to your home and execute everyone?"

Emma didn't answer.

My mouth went dry, and my hands trembled. I wrapped my arms around Izzie's waist, holding her steady on the table, offering her a weak smile.

What was Emma hiding?

The sheriff retrieved his phone from his pocket and scrolled through it before placing it on the table for Emma to view.

"Do you know what's on the video?" the sheriff asked.

Emma shook her head. She shifted on the metal chair, her head bent down, staring at the phone screen.

The sheriff presumably pushed play. I couldn't see the video, and the dialogue was too quiet to hear.

My fingers braided Izzie's hair, trying to distract myself from the weight of what happened through the glass. Maybe Izzie and I should have left. Emma had wanted us to be there to support her, but if she was involved, I wasn't sure I wanted to know about it.

"That's you on the surveillance footage," the sheriff said. "You were part of the team who took over the resort and held seventy-three people hostage."

Emma pursed her lips and folded her arms across her chest. "I was a victim."

"That's not what I see. What about this video?" He tapped his phone, and a moment later another clip played in the interrogation room.

Again, I couldn't hear what was said, but my chest ached as I found it harder to breathe.

"Tell me exactly what happened," the sheriff said, "and maybe we won't charge you with murder."

Silence filled the room for several long, drawn-out seconds before she finally cleared her throat to answer. "I always worked the front desk at Blue Sky Resort. It was my job to check in clients and take reservations. Imagine my surprise when one of the scout managers from Hollywood had booked a suite. I didn't plan any of it. You have to believe me."

He scribbled down notes as she spoke. "How did you know the client was a scout manager?"

"I used to live in Los Angeles. I worked for the studio and was a personal assistant to Mr. Joseph Kensington. He was my boss," Emma said. She exhaled a heavy sigh. "He was also an asshole, I might add. He liked to flirt with all the employees, including me. He told me to come into his office one time when the door was shut. He had a private bathroom and was whacking off when I walked in."

"So, you thought it would be a good idea to hold him hostage along with the other guests at the resort?"

Emma rubbed her eyes. "That wasn't my idea." She rested her hands on the table, tapping her fingers over the metal. "I mentioned to Ian about what my boss had done and how I'd been let go from my job. He told me no one else would get hurt. That his buddies would make sure Kensington never bothered anyone else. They were going to rough him up a little and then rob his hotel room. We figured there was probably a couple of grand in cash that he brought. It wasn't supposed to be a big deal. Ian took things too far."

"Does Ian have a last name?"

Her tongue darted out, swiping her top lips. "Yes. Ian Connor."

The air felt like it'd been sucked out of my lungs. Had Emma been in on the hostage takeover? The room spun, and I stumbled into the chair to sit down.

"Ella?" Izzie whispered, staring at me. She poked my cheek, seated above me on the table.

I reached for Isabella's hand and gave it a kiss. I didn't want to worry her. I tried to ignore Emma's voice from across the room, but it was pointless. I heard everything she said, and the more she spoke, the less remorseful she sounded.

"That still doesn't get us to the part about the men who attacked the compound, but I believe there may have been a correlation." The sheriff grabbed his file and flipped through, revealing a series of photographs. "Do you recognize any of these men?"

She pushed the file farther away, toward the sheriff. "No. Should I?"

"These were all hostages at the resort. Someone who might have a vendetta against their captors. Two of the men are known to work with a crime syndicate in Chicago." He flipped through the photographs and slid the picture across the table. "Take another look."

Emma exhaled loudly through her nose. "Yeah. I saw these two at the resort. They were sitting across from me in the hallway when I was being held with the other hostages, but they aren't the men who stormed the compound today."

"Did you see who did the shooting?"

"I didn't recognize them, but I did get a good long look at them right before I tore out on foot. They could have been friends with those guys." She tapped the picture. "But it wasn't them. Did you check the security footage from the compound?"

The sheriff slid back his chair, the feet squeaking with his movements. "What security footage?"

"Jayden set up cameras along the perimeter. I thought it was stupid and a waste of money, but maybe it can help you catch the men who did this?"

His eyes tightened. "I'm going to have a sketch artist work with you to recreate a representation of the men who targeted and attacked the compound. Can you do that for us?"

"Yeah, sure." Emma twirled her hair with her finger. "Can I get a bottle of water, something to eat? I'm famished."

I stood, unable to take any more of Emma's antics.

I bundled up Izzie in her winter coat and carried her out of the police station and down to my car. Thankfully, I had picked it up earlier that afternoon when Skylar had gone in to work.

I opened the back door and put her into the car seat that I had installed. Jaxson had a spare one in the house which had come in handy. After she was buckled, I climbed into the front seat, started the engine, and texted Skylar.

I'm taking Izzie with me to visit Mason. He's in the hospital. Will be home late.

I didn't further elaborate. If she had any questions, she could call me. I looked up the hospital where Mason had been brought and called them to ensure that he was able to have visitors.

Apparently, he'd been airlifted and transported to Sanford Health, a level one trauma center, over ten hours away from Breckenridge.

"Fuck!"

Izzie repeated my curse. "Fuck. Fuck. Fuck."

I exhaled a long, heavy sigh. Crap. I couldn't get mad at her; she didn't understand what she was doing when she repeated me. Hopefully, she'd stop saying 'fuck' before Jaxson returned home.

When would he be back?

Starting the car, I pulled out from the police station parking lot and headed home with Izzie. "I guess it's just you and me." At least until Skylar came home. I had a distinct impression that she didn't like me, but I wasn't sure why.

We drove back to Jaxson's home. Every part of me was exhausted. I was ready for bed but still needed to make dinner. I carried Izzie up to the house and put her down on the porch while I fished out my keys. As I grabbed them from my purse, my gaze landed on the door.

Shit.

The front door was ajar. I hadn't left it open. I'd locked it when I left, and there wasn't any sign of

Skylar. The alarm wasn't on, or at least it hadn't gone off from what I could surmise.

Had I remembered to turn it on when we left?

I hoisted Izzie into my arms and backed up, slamming into a man who had come up around the side of the house. I felt the barrel of his gun nestled in my back.

"Welcome home," he said, his voice calm and even, almost a little too friendly. Was it because I had Izzie in my arms?

"What do you want?" I guided Izzie down, planting her feet on the ground. I didn't want her to glance over my shoulder at the man pointing his weapon at me.

"Let's go inside and have a little chat."

Izzie stepped inside, and I slowly reached for the light, flipping it on. "Is that really necessary?" I asked, nodding toward the gun. "There's a child here. Do we absolutely need to give the girl nightmares?"

"Call the Eagle Tactical guy. What's his name?"

"I don't know what you're talking about," I said, playing dumb.

He stepped into the house behind me and shut the door. "Call your boss. Tell him Nikolai is here and wants a trade."

I slowly pulled out my phone and dialed Jaxson. "I don't know that he'll pick up the phone. He's out of town." I didn't want to elaborate on his flight or the details of the mission.

"Hey, we're just finishing up here in Chicago." His voice was cheery, carefree, and at ease. I wanted to ask if everything had gone well, but I couldn't, not with the stranger in the house.

I spoke slowly and clearly, doing my best not to panic. "Jaxson." At least the gun wasn't pointed at me anymore, which gave me the opportunity to fight back. The only problem was Izzie. I didn't want to risk her life. "You need to come home."

"What's wrong? Is Izzie all right?" Jaxson asked.

Nikolai hadn't laid so much as a hand on her, but it didn't mean he wouldn't. I'd protect her to the bitter end, but if I wasn't alive, what good was I to Izzie?

My gaze lifted from Izzie to the man holding us hostage in Jaxson's home. "It's Nikolai. He's here, and he wants a trade."

There was no answer.

"Jaxson?" I moved my phone from my ear to look at the screen. "Great," I muttered under my breath.

"What?" Nikolai asked as he stepped closer, brooding.

"The call dropped." I showed Nikolai my phone. I hadn't hung up, and I was confident Jaxson wouldn't have hung up the call, either.

"Call him back."

I had zero bars. "I don't have a signal."

Nikolai shoved his cell phone at me. "Call him," he demanded.

I dialed Jaxson's phone and breathed a sigh of relief when he picked up. "Ariella?"

"Yes. Nikolai is here. He has a message he wants me to give you."

Nikolai ripped the phone from my fingers, having lost his patience with me. "I know you have possession of my sister, Hazel."

He stared at me, his eyes raking over my body before glancing at Izzie.

"Bring her to me, or you'll be picking out a coffin for the little girl."

CHAPTER TWENTY-THREE

JAXSON

"I'll kill him!" I shouted, staring at my phone. The bastard threatened my daughter's life and then, like a coward, hung up.

Lincoln rested a hand on my arm. "We're not going to let anything happen to Izzie, and we know Ariella is with her. She'll protect her. What's the plan?"

I couldn't think straight. My heart slammed against the walls of my ribcage, trying to break free of its prison. I took off on foot for our car, parked on the other side of the blockade.

"Someone tipped Nikolai off," I said.

Lincoln, Hazel, and Aiden followed after me. Lincoln dug out the car keys for the rental car from his pocket, while Hazel kept up with my pace, walking alongside me.

"Do you think it was Franco?" Lincoln asked. He hit the button on the remote to unlock the doors.

I hustled to the car and climbed in.

"Doubtful," Hazel said. She opened the door and hopped into the backseat. "Franco was convinced that Nikolai had arranged a flight home when he found out I was back in Chicago. We were waiting for him to return home. I thought he was en route."

Lincoln and Aiden climbed into the car. Lincoln started the engine and tore out of the neighborhood for the airport.

"Who else knew you were in Chicago?" I asked and turned around so that I could face her. I didn't think she'd lie to me, but I also wasn't sure what the hell was going on anymore. Why the hell was Nikolai at my house threatening my daughter and Ariella?

"Does it matter?" Lincoln asked. "We need to come up with a plan. I'll call Declan and let him know what's going on. He can stake out your house. Maybe he'll be able to slip inside or at least know how many men we're up against."

"At least Nikolai and his driver, Sacha," Hazel said. "They go everywhere together. I'm surprised Nikolai didn't marry me off to him." She shifted in the back seat and stared out the window.

"Can you go any faster?" I asked, glaring at Lincoln. Traffic may not have been Lincoln's fault, but we definitely weren't taking the best route. I wasn't familiar with Chicago, but there had to be another way to get to the airport.

———

Driving to the airport had been tedious, but not as painstaking as the flight home. We had a private jet, but it didn't mean we arrived any quicker than flying commercial.

When we eventually landed, we texted Declan.

Flight landed. On our way. Please tell me you have good news.

I wanted the mission to be over with and Izzie and Ariella to be safe and the operation behind us. That was wishful thinking.

Declan didn't answer. We rushed off the plane and straight to my truck. I threw myself into the driver's side, not letting anyone else take the reins. It was hard not to crave control, especially when it was my own family on the line.

"Are you sure you don't want to call the sheriff and involve the local police?" Aiden asked from the backseat.

"No. We're doing this off the books."

In the backseat of Declan's truck, was a stash of weapons and supplies for us. It would keep us from having to make an extra stop at the Eagle Tactical office.

"Any word from Declan?" I asked. My phone was buried in my pocket, but I had group texted our message so that any of the guys could answer if he responded.

I glanced at Lincoln beside me in the front seat.

Lincoln pulled out his phone, viewed the texts, and then shook his head. "Nothing yet. Don't you have surveillance cameras with your security system?"

"They're disabled, along with the alarm system. I attempted to access the system while we were catching our flight, but I couldn't get into the Wi-Fi system."

"Do you think he cut the power?" Hazel asked.

"I don't know. There's a battery backup system, but he could have disabled that if he knew how to hack into the system. It looks like the system was disarmed and hacked."

I had hoped it was impenetrable, but Declan could have hacked it. I wasn't sure about Nikolai's abilities or the man who tagged along with him.

"My brother is a thug. He's good with a gun and having his men do his dirty work. Nikolai wouldn't know how to hack anything," Hazel said.

Maybe that should have made me feel better, but it didn't.

"Shit. I need to call Skylar and warn her not to come home right now." I didn't want to give Nikolai another hostage. He hadn't mentioned her, which meant she mustn't have been home.

I used voice dialing and waited for Skylar to answer. It went straight to voicemail. "Listen, don't come home right now. Something is going down at the house, and I need you to go to my office. There's a sofa. Crash there for the night."

I ended the call. My eyes narrowed as I focused on the road. I should have called Skylar earlier while I was in Chicago. If she was already home from work and I had given Nikolai a third hostage, I would never forgive myself.

We hurried up the mountain pass and down the gravel road for my house, closing in, drawing nearer. I cut the engine and shut the truck off a few yards away. I didn't want to alert Nikolai that we had arrived. We needed the upper hand.

With quiet precision, we snuck out of the truck and closed the doors, careful not to alert anyone inside of our arrival. I stalked past Nikolai's vehicle. The driver was slumped forward, dead.

Had Declan taken him out, or Nikolai? I'd find out later, right now I needed to get to our gear and rescue Izzie and Ariella.

Quietly, I pulled the door handle to Declan's vehicle and slid the equipment from the back seat and the floor, providing our team with guns and gear for the mission.

We needed to assume Nikolai was armed and prepared for our arrival. There was no chance that we were entering through the front door.

I took in my surroundings, listening for any signs of distress or other armed men who might have been watching. The river trickled to my east, but that was the only sound that reached my ears. With careful precision, we strode forward in silence, approaching the house.

Aiden followed behind me, with Lincoln in the rear. I wasn't crazy about Hazel coming with us, but if we didn't use her as bait, there was a higher chance that Nikolai would shoot my baby girl or Ariella. He wouldn't shoot Hazel; at least I was mostly confident he wouldn't hurt her.

There were no guarantees. He had sold her off to be married.

I held my breath on our approach, hugging the window as I listened for sounds inside and any indication of their whereabouts.

Aiden tapped me on the back, and I glanced over my shoulder. He pointed at the ground, the broken cell phone on the slushy packed snow that had begun to melt.

Declan's phone had been abandoned, the screen smashed. I tilted my head up to glance at the roof. Had he climbed atop and dropped his phone?

With a goofy grin, he waved down at us.

Bastard.

He was in position with his sniper rifle. While I appreciated that he made sure no other assholes were hidden in the forest and he had the upper hand, I also needed to get inside the house. Lying up on the roof wasn't going to help me rescue Izzie and Ariella.

We needed to find a way inside the house and not through the front door.

CHAPTER TWENTY-FOUR

ARIELLA

I had hours until Jaxson flew back from Chicago and arrived in Breckenridge. He wouldn't turn over Hazel to Nikolai in exchange for his daughter and my safety.

Nikolai wasn't an idiot. He had to suspect the same, which meant there had to be another power play he had. I just wasn't sure what he planned.

He had snatched my phone along with his cell phone, burying both in his pocket. Not that I was anticipating my captor would allow me another phone call.

"Why are you here?" I asked, staring him down. While he was quite a bit taller than I was, I didn't give the illusion that I was afraid of him.

Big mistake.

He smashed the barrel of the gun against my cheek and pushed me backward, stumbling over the toys on the living room floor.

I caught myself, but not before Nikolai lurched forward and shoved me onto the sofa.

"Sit," he commanded—a single word with the authority to send shivers down my spine.

Izzie came running toward me. His tone must have frightened her. "Come here," I said, holding out my arms as she climbed into my lap.

She clung tight against me, and while she hadn't been bothered earlier by the stranger, unaware of the danger, it seemed now she understood that we were in trouble.

Izzie's arms clung around my neck. I shifted her weight, having her sit on my lap, my arms wrapped around her, protective and comforting.

"Would you put that away?" I gestured toward the gun that he'd assaulted me with moments earlier. "All you're doing is scaring her." I didn't want to admit that I was scared too. He probably got off on frightening women.

Nikolai huffed under his breath and shoved the gun into the waistband of his pants. "Don't try anything stupid," he said. His eyes tightened, and he glanced Izzie and me over from head to toe.

I swallowed the bile rising in my throat, the fear pulsing through my veins, pumping like oxygen to my heart. He wasn't going to let us go, and given his history of bloodshed at the compound, I needed a plan.

Think.

I clung to Izzie, but that didn't settle the terror that rotted in my stomach like spoiled meat. A thin sheen of sweat coated my forehead. I wiped my brow and stared down at the floor. The last thing I wanted was to appear threatening.

Nikolai was in charge.

I needed to make myself small and insignificant. Not so much so that he'd kill me, but that he wouldn't find me threatening. What had all my training at the C.I.A. taught me?

I could disarm him, but that assumed there weren't others ready to shoot me the minute I opened the front door. Or worse, what if he discharged his gun and shot Izzie?

I couldn't live with myself if something happened to her. Jaxson would never forgive me, either.

Get inside his head.

What made him tick? What was his agenda? Without a doubt, he didn't just want to strut out with Hazel at his side and return to Chicago. No. He was a mobster with a thirst for blood.

If I asked him why he was doing this, he'd shut me out. I needed to dig deeper. I glanced at the clock. We had at least a few hours together. Could I get him to talk?

My mouth was dry, and my words came out raspy. "We're going to be here a while. Can I get up and grab a book to read to Izzie?" I asked. While I didn't budge from my position on the sofa, I pointed toward the bookshelf in the dining room, just behind us.

"You don't move," Nikolai said. He strode across the room in earnest and stood there for a fraction of a second before he yanked a book from the shelf. He shuffled back to the living room and towered above us. "Here." He tossed a soft lavender paperback book at me.

Alice's Adventures in Wonderland.

I was shocked that it was a children's book he found. He'd been so quick that I thought he had pulled the first book he'd found on the shelf.

"Thank you," I said and opened the book, starting with the first page. "Have you read this before?" I asked Izzie. Hopefully, it wasn't too old for her, but it was a classic.

She shook her head no.

"She'll like it." Nikolai paced the length of the room several times over before standing in the corner of the room, just a few feet away, watching us. He folded his arms across his chest. "Read it to her."

I flipped past the title page and opened to chapter one.

"Down the Rabbit-Hole," I said and read the heading for the first chapter, while Izzie wiggled her bottom and curled up in my arms.

Her body relaxed as I read, every word seeming to comfort her. Could it have been a simple fact that this was a distraction that made her feel better?

"Alice was beginning to get very tired of sitting by her sister on the bank and of having nothing to do; once or twice she had peeped into the book her sister was reading, but it had no pictures or conversations in it, 'and what is the use of a book,' thought Alice 'without pictures or conversations?'"

Izzie rested her hand against my chest, over my heart, as she closed her eyes. Envious that she could sleep through anything, including a mad man waving a gun at us. Well, for the moment, the gun was tucked into his pants, but it was within his reach.

I kept reading, page by page. Her body slumped as she fell asleep in my arms. A sigh of relief fell past my lips and spilled out as I finished the second chapter.

"Keep reading," Nikolai demanded of me.

I did as he said, only because he flashed his gun at me, threatening both of our lives if I didn't do as he commanded.

Every so often, I glanced up as I read in a soft, hushed whisper to find a strange semblance of something familiar cross Nikolai's face.

"You've read this before," I said. The only solution was to get him to open up and talk. If I could find a way that related to him, maybe he'd spare our lives.

"We're not talking," Nikolai said. His finger gestured for me to turn the page and continue reading.

Avoiding conflict, I didn't shut the book. However, I also didn't do what he wanted. I kept the page unturned, the book open, my eyes wide as I stared up at Nikolai. "Your sister, Hazel, is quite a bit younger than you."

While I didn't know how old Nikolai was, he had years weathered to his skin, his brow, his hands, and neck. Stress aged a person; so did murder.

He didn't stop me, but he also didn't comment on my observation.

"Did you read this book to Hazel when she was little?" I asked. Could I conjure the good memories, and he'd come to his senses?

He pushed himself away from the corner of the room, his arms still folded against his chest, protective in nature. At the moment, he wasn't trying to scare me or wake Izzie. He paced the length of the room, back and forth, his jaw tight.

Nikolai's hands fell to his sides, his hands bunched into fists. "I read that book to my sister, but it wasn't Hazel."

"You have another sister?" Had she too been sold and married off to another mobster? I held my tongue; it wasn't an appropriate question to ask if I wanted him to open up and find a way out of this disaster.

I needed to act with stealth. I had to be sneaky if I was going to interrogate him without him even realizing that's what I was doing.

His bottom lip jutted out, and his top lip tightened. A tic coursed through him once, forcing his eyes to soften. As quickly as it happened, he grunted and shuffled his feet, pacing louder.

Please don't wake Izzie.

He couldn't read my mind. Not that I expected him to, I just didn't want her to be frightened again. She deserved some peaceful slumber free of nightmares. I wasn't sure I'd be so lucky if I survived today.

"Yes, I had a baby sister before Hazel. Her name was Rebecca." Something flashed behind his gaze, a flicker that made me believe he wasn't always the monster he'd become.

"You used to read *Alice's Adventures in Wonderland* to her?" I needed to make him see the connection, the familiarity, and maybe then he wouldn't put Izzie in harm's way. If only he realized her innocence and that she was an innocent child.

He stopped pacing and hovered above us.

I shivered from his presence, from his brooding nature that made me feel tiny and insignificant.

Nikolai reached toward me, and I shuddered from fear.

He grabbed the throw blanket on the back of the sofa and unfolded it, placing it over Izzie as she slept.

The warmth comforted me too. Was he not the monster everyone believed him to be? I didn't know how I could ask him if he had shot everyone in the compound without him turning defensive and building up a wall.

"Thank you," I whispered, staring up at him.

He grunted and stepped back, his nostrils flaring as he breathed heavily in and out of his nose.

"Are you and Rebecca still close?" I asked. I had to keep asking questions to understand what he was doing and maybe find a way out.

Nikolai's gaze grew dark. "She's dead."

Not another word was spoken. He didn't elaborate on how she died or when.

"I'm sorry." I had meant it; whether he realized it or not, losing a sibling was hell. I hadn't lost my sister, not physically, but emotionally, we'd fallen apart. I'd lost a child, and that had been heart-wrenching.

He stared at me long and hard before giving a once-over nod. "Yeah. Me too. Cost of being in the family business," Nikolai said. He gave a shrug as if it didn't matter anymore and was all in the past.

"There doesn't have to be a cost. You don't have to keep killing people," I whispered.

His feet slammed against the floor as he whipped out his gun and pointed it at my head. "Shut it!"

I'd gone too far.

I closed my lips and let my gaze fall down to the floor. I held Izzie asleep in my arms. "Let me put her upstairs in bed."

"No."

I needed to protect her, but I couldn't do that with the barrel of a gun against my forehead.

If I died, who would protect Izzie? Jaxson would when he arrived, but how much longer until that happened? I couldn't let her get hurt. I wouldn't. Jaxson had been there for me, rescued me. I owed him my life. Now I was repaying the favor.

"She doesn't need to be involved in this, Nikolai. This is between you and me."

He rolled his eyes and cocked the safety off on the gun. "No."

A single word. That's all he said, and I could argue until my last breath. But what good would that do Izzie?

"Fine." I didn't argue. It wouldn't do any good. I needed to get him to continue to open up to me. He wasn't going to do that with his gun poised and ready to shoot. "I'm sorry," I said, apologizing. "You're in charge."

"Damn right, I'm in charge!" he growled.

I didn't move. I didn't flinch. I needed him to see that I wasn't a threat, and maybe then he'd put away the gun.

Silence enveloped the room.

My heart pounded against my chest. Could he hear the fear, the adrenaline coursing through my veins?

His breathing was heavy and loud, filling the quiet space.

After several minutes, he pulled his gun away from my forehead, put the safety back on, and shoved the weapon into the waistband of his pants.

My eyes shut, relieved he wasn't pointing his pistol at me. We still weren't done. I wasn't safe until he was in handcuffs and carted off to jail. Had Jaxson phoned the local sheriff?

I hadn't heard sirens, but maybe they were smart enough not to alert us of their presence?

My voice soft and timid, I needed answers. "What's going to happen to Hazel?"

Nikolai had made it clear that he wanted his sister returned to him. While I didn't think he'd let Izzie or me go, I wasn't sure what he planned to do with his sister.

"Why do you care?" He paced the length of the living room again, glancing every so often out the window. When he seemed satisfied that it was still just the three of us in the house, he returned his attention to me.

"I consider Hazel a friend."

The truth was I didn't have many friends. I'd alienated everyone in New York when my ex-husband had been convicted on multiple felony counts for embezzlement and fraud. Emma had been a friend, but that had been short-lived.

Nikolai strode over to the fireplace, examining the photographs on the mantle. "She doesn't have any friends."

I didn't know if that was true or not, but she seemed close to Mason, a secret I would take to my grave. There was no reason that Nikolai needed to know about him.

"I saved her life at the resort," I said.

"You were at the resort when those bastards came in and took hostages?" Nikolai rushed at me, the gun back out of his pants and now in his hand. He shoved it up under my jaw.

"I was a hostage, same as Hazel," I said. Did he think I was involved? Would he kill me because I spoke about the situation?

He appeared unhinged. Should I have been surprised?

"But you got her out?"

"It wasn't just me. I had help from the Eagle Tactical team." I didn't point out that I was employed by them. I wasn't sure whether he'd kiss me or kill me.

He snorted. "Those bastards betrayed me. When they show up with Hazel, they're dead. Every last one of them, including the little girl."

"No one is touching my little girl," Jaxson's voice echoed through the house, loud and clear.

I glanced over my shoulder for Jaxson.

I could have sworn he was behind me, but he wasn't in the house.

Nikolai backed away from me and glanced out the window, satisfied that Jaxson hadn't arrived yet. "Nice try!" he shouted.

His gun poised at the alarm speaker system, he fired off a round, blowing the plastic into tiny shards that shattered around the room.

CHAPTER TWENTY-FIVE

JAXSON

"I'm going in there with you," Hazel demanded as we breached the property.

I didn't have time to argue. While I wasn't keen on another hostage, she was also the bait. The one thing that Nikolai wanted, and the only way to ensure Izzie's safety along with Ariella's, was to dangle the carrot in front of the rabbit.

"Stay out of the way," I warned. We had climbed in through the back window in the bathroom, and Declan had hacked into the security system through the wiring outside to offer a distraction.

I snuck inside the house through the window.

Declan stayed on the roof, keeping a lookout while Aiden and Lincoln followed behind me.

Hazel was in the rear, with no weapons, but she did have a bulletproof vest on to protect her.

Nikolai wouldn't shoot his own sister, would he?

Declan played my recording that we'd made a few minutes earlier outside over the speaker system attached to the alarm.

While the alarm had been disabled, it hadn't been destroyed. "No one is touching my little girl." It was strange to hear my own voice and dangerous to alert him of our arrival, but we had to do something.

From the window, I'd seen the bastard with a gun positioned on Ariella's forehead.

I couldn't take the chance that he'd shoot her or Izzie.

I kept my head down; they'd be looking for the team and for me.

"Nice try!" Nikola's voice shouted through the downstairs of the house. A single shot rang out as Nikolai pointed the gun at the speaker and blew it away.

We came around from the kitchen, Ariella's back to me, the sofa pointed toward the front door.

"Freeze!" I shouted, my gun drawn and poised on Nikolai.

Aiden and Lincoln held their firearms up, three men versus one.

"Don't even think about it," Lincoln said. "Put your gun down slowly."

"Give me Hazel and I'll walk away. You'll never have to see me again," Nikolai said. He held up his gun in a surrender maneuver.

I didn't trust him. We'd heard from Declan that the sheriff had received a call about the compound being shot up by two mafia fellows. One was inside my house, the other, I assumed was the dead man in the vehicle out on my driveway.

"That's not how this works," I said. I kept my gun trained on him as he came around into the living room, blocking Izzie and Ariella.

Aiden pulled out his handcuffs that he'd attached to his belt. "Put the gun down slowly. Arms up."

Nikolai held one arm up in surrender and the other, he slowly guided down.

The front door handle jiggled open, grabbing our attention. Who the hell was on the other side of the door? Declan was supposed to be up on the roof still.

Skylar pulled the door open and stepped inside, coming face to face with Nikolai.

With his free hand, he reached for Skylar, yanked her against him and gripped her hair, shoving the barrel of the gun against her neck.

"Let me go!" Skylar screamed.

"Daddy!" Izzie shrieked in terror.

I couldn't turn around and look back at my little girl and assure her everything was all right. My focus had to be on the monster standing just a few feet away from me, with my sister as his hostage.

Skylar had no formal tactical training. She'd never been in the military or spent a day doing self-defense. I couldn't count on her to get out of his clutches.

"You don't have to do this, Nikolai," Hazel said. She trailed out from around the hallway and came up beside Lincoln and grabbed his spare gun from his holster at his hip. She pointed the gun at herself, lifting it to her temple.

"Hazel, what are you doing?" Nikolai's eyes grew wide, and his voice was frantic. "Think about what you're doing, sis."

"If you kill her," Hazel said, her voice quivered as she spoke, "you'll never see me again."

With my gun trained on Nikolai, I couldn't stop Hazel from doing something stupid. I didn't know her well enough to determine if she was bluffing, but I couldn't take the chance. "You don't want to do that, Hazel."

"Yes, I do." Hazel nodded, her hand trembling with the gun poised against her skin, the barrel flush with her body. She might have been wearing a bulletproof vest, but it wouldn't save her, not with what she had planned.

"Listen to your sister," Lincoln said. "She's willing to die because of what you did."

Skylar struggled against Nikolai, squirming in his grasp, trying to shrug away from him, but he wouldn't let her escape.

"Let me go," Skylar whispered, her eyes welled with tears. "Please. I don't even know what's going on. I won't tell anyone."

I wasn't going to let him disappear. Not after all that he'd done. "Tell Hazel what you did, Nikolai."

Nikolai shook his head, his dark, thick hair falling into his eyes. "Everything I've done was for you, Hazel. All I wanted was your happiness."

"My happiness?" Hazel scoffed and stepped forward, her own gun still pointed at her head. "You sold me to Franco to be his bride! I'd sooner die than marry that disgusting pig."

Nikolai blinked several times over; his expression looked perplexed. "What?"

"You heard me!" Hazel shouted as she stepped closer, unafraid of her brother. "I'm tired of you running my life and ruining it. I know what you and Dad did. I know about the jobs, the fake agency I worked for, the boyfriends you and Dad paid off. I'm not an idiot, you know."

Nikolai released his grip on Skylar, and she hurried away from him as Lincoln grabbed her and dragged her behind him for protection.

"They weren't good enough for you," Nikolai said, his attention on Hazel. "It's my duty to protect you. You're my baby sister. Those men weren't deserving of you."

"You bastard, that was my decision to make!" Hazel shouted up at him. As she stared him down, the gun trembled in her grip, her finger on the trigger.

Nikolai lowered the gun in his hand and reached for Hazel's weapon. "If you die, I'll kill every last one of them."

"No, you won't," Hazel said and turned the gun, pulling the trigger, and shooting Nikolai in the chest.

CHAPTER TWENTY-SIX

Hazel

I'd done it for them, everyone he'd ever killed, tortured, or hurt.

I turned the gun from my own forehead to his chest. It'd been reckless, without thought or calculation. He could have easily shot me with his gun in retaliation. I wouldn't have blamed him if he had.

My finger squeezed the trigger. It was the only way to put an end to what he'd done.

I couldn't go home again. Nikolai would never stop hunting me down, demanding that I do as he wanted because we were blood.

Franco had been arrested, but with the head of the mafia dead, another leader would rise from the ashes, and I would be forgotten. At least I hoped I would be forgotten.

The room spun; the world felt like it was moving in slow motion.

Lincoln kicked the gun away from Nikolai as he lay on the floor, bleeding out.

I stumbled several steps backward before hitting a warm body. Jaxson removed the gun from my hands. I felt cold and empty, alone.

"I'm sorry," Jaxson said into my ear. The cold, rough metal of handcuffs clasped onto my wrists as he secured them behind my back.

"I understand." I expected nothing less. They'd cart me off to jail. I'd be going to prison for a long time.

"Are handcuffs really necessary?" Lincoln shot Jaxson a glance.

"It's just a formality," Jaxson said. "I need to know that my family is no longer in any danger. I'll call the sheriff and let him know what happened."

Aiden bent down to Nikolai lying on the floor.

Blood pooled around Nikolai, his skin pale, his eyes closed. I didn't have the courage to ask if he was still breathing.

I wanted to kill Nikolai after all he'd done to destroy my life, but I'd never believed myself to be a murderer. Guilt weighed heavily on me. I'd acted in self-defense, not only for my own life but of those around me.

Nikolai would never have let any of them go.

Jaxson made a quick phone call to the sheriff while I sat on the floor beside my brother. His skin looked cold, but I couldn't touch him, my hands behind my back.

Aiden pressed against the wound, attempting to stop the flow of blood oozing out of the wound. With his other hand, he felt for a pulse and shook his head. "He's dead."

I collapsed onto my knees, staring down at my brother. Stepbrother or not, he was still family. Blood was blood.

"You're with Rebecca now. It's better that way," I whispered, staring down at Nikolai. I had never met Rebecca, his biological sister. He'd spoken of her greatly when we were younger, how her life had been cut short, murdered by another gangster. It had driven our father to become the head of the mafia, to rise up in retaliation.

I wanted it to be over, all of it. The carnage. The slayings. The killing for blood.

———

I'd given my statement to the local sheriff. The team from Eagle Tactical had given their statements, as had Ariella. We had been taken individually into a room, questioned, and then asked to provide in writing what happened.

I confessed to shooting Nikolai.

It seemed Nikolai had also killed his driver, Sacha, though I had no answer as to why.

I had expected to spend the rest of my life in prison, but the handcuffs came off, and I was free to go.

The D.A. wasn't going to press charges.

Had Nikolai been alive, he would have been charged with multiple counts of murder after raiding the compound and killing dozens of men, women, and children.

I thought I might vomit when the sheriff informed me what my brother had done in retribution for the resort. It was all over.

I headed out of the police station, surprised to find Ariella waiting for me.

"I never did thank you properly," Ariella said. She leaned against her sedan, her hands in her jacket pockets. "If you hadn't offered yourself as you did, I don't know how we would have gotten out of that situation."

I shrugged. "It was nothing." I didn't want her to make a big deal of it. "Have you heard anything about Mason?"

I wanted to see him, to make sure he was all right, and thank him for saving my life. He was one of the reasons that I was still standing, alive, and breathing.

"We've already chartered a flight to Fargo to visit him in the hospital. Do you want to come with us?" Ariella asked.

"Yes. I need to see him and thank him for what he did for me."

————

I hurried down the hospital corridor.

Would Mason even want to see me? His Uncle Jeb died because of me.

If I wouldn't have requested his help, his uncle would still be alive, and Mason wouldn't have been shot.

The smell of antiseptic burned my nostrils. I paused in the empty waiting room.

"Do you mind staying here with Izzie?" Jaxson asked Ariella.

"Sure," she said as she smiled and took the toddler from her father's arms.

I opened my mouth to offer to watch the little girl for Jaxson but thought better of it. I wasn't great with kids, and I wanted to see Mason. I was worried he wouldn't be happy to see me.

Lincoln and Jaxson headed through the doors and down the corridor. I hesitated before following, several feet behind them. They talked amongst one another. I was the outsider, and while they hadn't tried to exclude me, I wasn't one of them.

What was I doing here? I felt out of place.

Lincoln and Jaxson headed into the private room without so much as a knock. I hung out in the hallway, trying to find the courage to enter.

I could handle shoving a gun against my own head, but stepping five feet forward into a hospital room was too much. That, apparently, was my limit.

"How's Hazel?" Mason's voice was raspy and rough.

He couldn't see me, as I was just right outside his room, but I could hear the sweet sound of his voice. It was filled with concern for me.

I hugged the wall, my back against the cold, white brick.

"She could tell you herself if she came in here," Lincoln said.

"She's here?" Mason asked. The sheets rustled and the hospital bed creaked. "Hazel?"

I shut my eyes. I couldn't hide forever. He'd know I was avoiding him if I didn't storm into his room and greet him right now.

"Hey." I mustered the best smile that I could as I stepped into his hospital room. "I was just out in the hallway looking for flowers I could steal for you."

Mason smiled and laughed, grimacing.

"Does it hurt to laugh?" I asked, worried about him. I came up alongside his bed.

"It's worth it," Mason said. He reached for my hand, our fingers intertwining. "Sit with me."

I didn't want to tell him there wasn't room. He was injured, but if he wanted my company, how could I say no? He'd only been shot because of me.

"How are you feeling?" I asked, sitting on the edge of the hospital bed by his side. "Any news when you will be released?"

"The doctor says that I can be discharged into someone's care at home, or else I have to go to a rehab facility." His eyes never left mine. "You owe me one, Hazel."

I laughed under my breath. "Don't beat around the bush." I couldn't believe he was playing the fact that I owed him.

Of course, I owed him, but I didn't think he was the kind of guy who would have collected on it.

"Please, will you stay with me?"

I hadn't thought about where I'd go now that Nikolai was dead and Franco was in prison. Mason needed me, though, and I genuinely liked him. I hadn't felt that way for anyone else, ever. It had always been him since we were teenagers.

"Well, since you asked nicely," I said and gave a weak smile. I wanted to stay, but I wanted it to be because he wanted me in his life, not just as his caretaker. Leaning down, I planted a soft, chaste kiss on his forehead.

"Is that all I get? What's a guy got to do to get a real kiss around here, die?"

My eyes widened in horror.

"Bad joke?" Mason smiled with that boyish grin that made my heart flutter and knees weak. I leaned in and brushed my lips over his.

The heart monitor started beeping faster.

Jaxson stood by the window of the room, a smile on his face. "Don't kill him. We still need him as part of our team. Speaking of the team, Lincoln, I'm going to offer you full time again. I know your restaurant will be undergoing renovations. Is there any way we can talk you into joining us? Don't make me beg."

"I'm not even dead yet and you're replacing me," Mason said. He laughed and grimaced.

I rested a gentle hand on his good arm, hoping to settle him back down. "I'm sure they're not replacing you," I said.

"I wouldn't be too sure," Lincoln said. "I'll do it, at least for now. It'll be a while until the check comes through from insurance, and then I'll have to decide what I'm going to do."

"I'm sorry about your restaurant," I said, smiling weakly at Lincoln. If I hadn't gone to his restaurant that morning, maybe the thugs who wanted me dead wouldn't have shot up the place.

Lincoln's jaw was tight, and he leaned against the wall near the foot of the hospital bed. "Don't mention it. These guys have been bugging me for the past several years to join Eagle Tactical. They're probably happy about what happened."

"Happy is a strong word," Mason said, "but ecstatic, yes."

Lincoln rolled his eyes.

Jaxson headed past Lincoln and gestured for him to follow out of the room. "We'll leave you two to talk. We'll be in the waiting room with Ariella and Izzie. Let us know if you need anything," Jaxson said.

"Thank you for coming. Hopefully, they'll spring me out of here soon," Mason said.

I waited until the other guys were gone and down the hall.

"Something on your mind?" Mason asked.

"I'm sorry for everything." I leaned down, planting my lips on his, hungrily taking a taste.

Having almost lost him, had torn me up inside. I'd already lost my brother at my own hands. I couldn't lose the man I'd loved since I was a teenager.

Mason reached out and his thumb stroked my cheek as my chin rested in his palm. "You have nothing to apologize for, but I do know one thing you could do to help me feel better after we get out of here."

"Anything," I said. "I'm all yours. Whatever you need, Mason, I'm here for you." I meant it too. I'd do whatever he needed me to do to care for him, whether it involved changing bandages or making him meals.

"Any chance you have a cute little nurse's outfit? As long as you're going to be taking care of me, I thought we could do a little fantasy roleplay."

CHAPTER TWENTY-SEVEN

ARIELLA

I sat with Izzie in the waiting room, letting her watch a video on my smartphone. We kept the audio down so that we wouldn't bother any hospital patients.

Having lost track of time, I hadn't seen Jaxson approach us.

"How are my two favorite ladies?" Jaxson asked.

"Daddy!" Izzie jumped down from my lap and held up her arms for her daddy to lift her up.

Jaxson picked her up and twirled her around before holding her on his hip. "We'll be leaving soon, hopefully. It sounds like Mason's going to get sprung out of here today, as long as he has someone at home."

"Oh?" I didn't know if he lived alone or had roommates. I hadn't heard him talk about dating anyone, but it was obvious he had the hots for Hazel. Anyone could see it.

"Hazel is going to stay and help him out," Jaxson said.

"That's good." I was happy for her, thrilled that maybe the two of them could figure out their relationship with time and wouldn't have to hide it from everyone. Albeit a little jealous too, but I would never admit it to anyone.

Lincoln stood a few feet away, at the vending machine making himself a cup of coffee.

"I was worried about you," Jaxson said and sat down beside me in the empty chair. He reached out and brushed a strand of hair behind my ear. "Still am worried if I'm to be honest."

I smiled weakly. I couldn't stop thinking about Nikolai.

What Hazel had done, the blood, the fact Nikolai had done everything to protect his sister. It had been messed up and sick, but it didn't detract from the fact he was dead. "I'm fine." I wanted to be fine, telling myself and saying it aloud.

Would it make it true?

"Are you sure?" he asked, his hand falling to my back.

I relaxed under his touch as he softly caressed my back in soothing motions. I wanted him to touch me, to kiss me, to make love to me.

Lincoln was in the room, and we were supposed to be keeping our relationship a secret if we were going to be together.

I shook my head no. "I'll probably have nightmares for a while, but it's nothing I can't handle."

Lincoln's heavy footsteps broke the spell and moment between the two of us. "Can I get you guys a coffee? The machine isn't working. I'm going to go down to the cafeteria. Want anything?"

"I'm good," I said.

"Me too," Jaxson said.

Lincoln headed down the hallway and the opposite direction of Mason's room for the elevator to the lobby where the cafeteria was located.

We had a few minutes, just the two of us, plus Izzie. Thankfully, she didn't seem to grasp what was going on between us.

Jaxson put Izzie on the seat beside him and played a video on his phone, letting her watch it. He stalked to the vending machine and gestured for me to come over to him.

I stood and stretched before I pointed at the machine. "Didn't you hear Lincoln? The coffee machine isn't working."

"I heard. I just wanted a little privacy." With Izzie's back to us, he pulled me against him, tight and hard.

My eyes widened as his lips descended onto mine, his fingers at the nape of my neck, keeping me close. It wasn't hard to melt into his kiss, my body falling easily under his spell.

He pulled back, one hand still on my neck, the other sliding under my shirt, teasing the waistband of my pants. "Jaxson," I said, smiling from the pleasure but warning him to stop. We couldn't be doing this in the hospital, let alone five feet away from his daughter.

"Lincoln will be a few minutes, and Hazel is preoccupied with Mason. I'll bet they're making out."

"Good for them," I said. That wasn't a reason that we should be doing that here and now. I gently rested a hand against his chest. "I want to be with you, but today was a lot."

"You know that I would never have let anything happen to you and Izzie?" Jaxson said.

"I know and I appreciate what you did today. It could have ended a lot differently," I said. The thoughts still flashed through my mind of Nikolai with his gun pressed against my forehead. I had to push those thoughts aside, or I wouldn't be able to breathe.

His lips came down hard on mine again, bruising, with a fierce intensity filled with want and need, not solely desire.

He shifted us around, my back against the wall as he pushed his knee between my thighs, hitting my center, my heat. I let him kiss me, and while I wanted to be more than just his secret girlfriend, I also was willing to accept whatever he gave.

My lips parted, drinking him in, pulling him tighter against me. Every thought from my mind disappeared as we kissed, and time seemed to stand still.

Someone cleared his throat rather loudly. Was he trying to get our attention?

I whimpered in protest when Jaxson pulled away, and we both glanced at the intruder, Lincoln.

He held his cup of coffee in his hand and took a long, slow sip. "Why don't the three of you get out of here?" Lincoln said. "I'll drive with Mason and Hazel to pick up his truck."

"Are you sure?" Jaxson asked.

"You have a ten-hour drive home. Izzie doesn't need to be kept out any later than necessary. I'll probably end up renting a hotel for the night and driving back tomorrow if Mason doesn't get released soon," Lincoln said.

Jaxson's cell phone rang, and he hurried over to grab it from Izzie as she watched her movie.

I stood awkwardly, giving Lincoln a weak smile. He'd been good to me, I had no complaints, but I still wasn't happy that he knew our secret. "Listen, what you saw—"

"It's none of my business," Lincoln said. "You make him happy, and I can honestly say there aren't too many people other than Izzie who can do that."

"You won't say anything to the others?" I hoped he could keep it to himself and not mention it to his buddies.

"Again, it's not my place," Lincoln said. He stepped closer. "You don't have to worry, Ariella. I like having you around. You're good for Jaxson, and you make him happy. That's all that matters."

I breathed a sigh of relief. "Thank you."

Jaxson hung up the phone and shoved it into his pocket.

"Daddy, phone." Izzie reached for his pants, trying to retrieve his phone.

"Not right now," he said and lifted his little one into his arms, giving her kisses. He shot a look at Lincoln. "Can you give Mason a message?"

Lincoln sipped his coffee. "Sure, what's up? Is everything okay?"

"The sheriff called to let us know they found his uncle's dog, Bear. They're keeping her at the station until someone comes to pick her up. Thankfully, she was all right, with a few scratches but no significant injuries. I let him know Mason was being released soon, but we're in Fargo, so it probably won't be until tomorrow."

"He'll be relieved to know Bear is all right," Lincoln said. "Text me the sheriff's number, and I'll make sure we pick up Bear on the way home."

———

It was a long drive back to Breckenridge. Jaxson insisted on being the one to drive. Izzie had fallen asleep an hour into the ride. It was dark and late, which probably helped her fall right to sleep.

"What's going to happen to Hazel?" I asked.

"You heard the sheriff; they don't plan on charging her with any crime because they closed the investigation and ruled it self-defense," Jaxson said.

"That's not what I'm talking about. Franco is still out there."

"He's in prison," Jaxson said. He glanced at me and reached for my hand as he drove.

Our fingers intertwined together. I gave his hand a squeeze, trying to reassure myself as much as him that I was okay. I didn't feel like myself. I still felt disconnected, lost in the events of the day.

"You don't worry that he'll come after you and your family?" I asked.

"If I worried about that, I'd be worrying about every bad guy we deal with," Jaxson said. He kept his voice low, careful not to wake Izzie. "Declan is fixing the security system and finding out how Nikolai managed to disable it."

Hearing that from Jaxson, I wanted to feel at ease. I wanted Franco to leave Hazel alone along with the rest of us. I squeezed his hand. "I guess it's just been a long day. Emma came to the house this morning, barefoot and hysterical."

"Nikolai shot up the compound where she's been living," Jaxson said.

"You knew she was living there? How?" I asked.

He let out a soft sigh, his focus and attention on the road as he spoke. "When I paid Ian and Seth a visit for harassing you, I discovered that she was living there. I had hoped she'd move out and come to her senses."

"She was involved in the hostage takeover at the resort," I said.

"I know."

I pulled my hand back as though I'd been burned. "How the hell did you know that? How many secrets have you been keeping?"

He placed his hand back on the steering wheel, his jaw tight. "More than I care to admit."

"What does that mean, Jaxson?" I couldn't believe he'd been hiding from me that he knew Emma had been involved in the hostage ordeal at Blue Sky Resort.

He let out a heavy sigh and glanced in the rearview mirror. "Can we have this conversation later?"

"No. I want to have the conversation now."

He'd been pissed when I'd kept secrets from him. How come he could keep secrets from me?

CHAPTER TWENTY-EIGHT

JAXSON

I wasn't thrilled that I'd been keeping *him* a secret, and now that we'd unleashed the fact Emma had been an off-gridder and was involved in the grim situation at the resort, it was bound to come out.

"Are you just going to ignore me?" Ariella asked. Her tone was sharp. She was undoubtedly pissed at me.

Great.

I had several hours left until we got to Breckenridge and home. It wasn't like I could drop her off and not see her again until work; we lived together.

I ran a hand through my hair, frustrated. Ariella tended to bring me down to my knees. "I'm not ignoring you; I've just got a lot on my mind."

"That's an excuse," Ariella said. She was pissed. I could hear her heavy, labored breathing as she shifted in her seat. She'd never get comfortable at this rate.

"Fine. You want every secret I've been keeping?" My voice raised in the confines of the truck. "I heard from one of the guys, and guess who was released from prison. Benjamin Ryan."

Ariella was dead silent.

"What? Don't you have something to shout at me for keeping that a secret? He's out of prison, Ariella. Do you know why?"

I glanced at her to see her eyes wide. Her mouth hung agape. I didn't let it go. If she wanted to know my secrets, I'd reveal hers, ones she didn't even know she had in the back of her closet.

"His convictions were overturned, every last one of them," I said. From the look on her face, she had no idea.

"You mentioned that he might not have been guilty. I just couldn't believe it was true." She ran her palms over her pants.

"Well, true or not, he's been released, and it's not on a technicality. I don't know what that means in regard to the C.I.A., whether they set him up or someone else." The truth was I hadn't had time to dig deeper or look into the mess of her past. "He made a statement on television when he was released."

"He did?" Her voice caught in her throat.

"Said something in the interview about planning on finding you," I said, a bitter taste filling my mouth.

I didn't want to lose her to *him*, her husband, or technically ex-husband. They were divorced, but if it had been based on the fact she'd believed he'd been guilty, and he wasn't, where did I stand?

What chance did I have against a wealthy man who had won her heart?

She exhaled a loud breath. "Well, if you see him, tell him to stay the hell away from me."

That took me by surprise. "What?"

Was she over him?

Did I not need to worry that he'd come and sweep her off her feet?

I wasn't one to get jealous easily, but I also didn't like to worry that a man with whom she had a history could breeze back into her life.

"He may not be guilty of the financial crimes that he was originally convicted of, but he's not innocent, Jaxson. Far from it."

What other crimes had he done that he hadn't been convicted of?

"Are you going to elaborate?" I asked.

Ariella yawned in the front seat. It was well past two in the morning. I recognized that she was drained. I was too. "Not tonight. I'm tired, Jaxson. Can we just leave it alone for now?"

Exhausted, I drove into the night, not wanting to crash in some shitty motel with bedbugs.

I didn't want to fight with her. I'd almost lost her and my daughter today. I rested my hand on her thigh. "I care about you, Freckles." I wanted her to know how

I felt. I didn't say it often enough, and she deserved to hear it from me.

"I know," she mumbled. Ariella rested her head against the side window, her eyes shut. Her breathing had lulled after several long seconds.

She mumbled something unintelligible. Had she just said *I love you?*

"Freckles?"

She'd fallen asleep.

Mason had once told me that he suspected her marriage might have been a cover, that she'd gone deep as a C.I.A. operative, too deep. If that was true, why had she been watching him, and what made her decide to marry him? If it hadn't been love, what was the catalyst?

There were secrets between us, but I wasn't willing to give her up, not without a fight.

Truth was that I loved her too.

Did I have the courage to tell her?

EPILOGUE

HARPER

I needed my caffeine fix if I was going to survive in this small, podunk town for the next few weeks.

My flight was short but choppy in the air and the stewardess had spilled my drink all over the seat in front of me. The poor bastard wore my coffee but that didn't solve my problem. I never got my drink on the flight.

I headed straight from the airport to the nearest coffee shop in Breckenridge. I prayed that they had a cafe that served a decent latte.

I doubted anyone would even recognize me, which played to my advantage. Plus, the giant sunglasses didn't hurt. This way, I didn't have to worry about reporters stalking me or fans snapping photos with their cell phone cameras.

It was early, the sun had come up recently and I strolled in, my mood more chipper than even I was prepared for on this early Sunday morning.

"Tall latte with caramel and whipped cream." I was going all out this morning.

The girl behind the counter in her brown apron and matching hat didn't so much as smile. "What's the name?" she asked. Her name tag read *Skylar*.

Did she really not recognize me? "Harper." I almost thought of giving her my real name or even a fake name, wouldn't that be fun?

She squinted slightly, as if she was deciding whether to believe me or not as I paid in cash.

"It'll be just a minute." Her tone was monotonous as she faked a smile.

"Next!" Skylar snapped, taking the order of the woman behind me.

I took a step back from the register and sat down at a nearby table. The place wasn't overly crowded and the longer I waited, the more impatient I became.

The woman behind me was given her coffee along with two other patrons after I had ordered. "What the hell?" I muttered under my breath. Had she forgotten about my order?

A handsome gentleman, tall with thick muscles and tattoos that peeked out from his sleeves, stole my attention for a minute as he ordered. He seemed to brighten Skylar's mood too.

I was going to change that. She'd ruined my mood and my good morning. "Excuse me," I said, interrupting the two of them. I'd had enough waiting. "I ordered a coffee ten minutes ago."

"It's been five," Skylar snapped. "And your drink is on the counter waiting for you to pick it up."

I glanced at the counter as she casually placed the cup in my view. It hadn't been waiting for me to grab it. She'd kept it hidden. That snotty brat!

"You didn't call my name."

She pointed at the cup and the name written on it. "Heather."

I swallowed the lump in my throat. There was no way she knew that was my real name. "It's Harper," I corrected her.

"Same difference. Do you want your coffee or not?"

Ten minutes. That coffee had to be cold and gross. I liked my coffee piping hot. I didn't pay nearly ten dollars for a shitty cup of coffee. "You need to make me another latte." I wasn't going to accept this kind of crappy treatment from an overpriced cafe.

A second barista on the other side of the counter poured a cup of steaming hot coffee and secured a lid. "Lincoln," she called out.

Oh hell no. That was mine. I snatched the cup before Lincoln could get his monstrous bear claws on it. He was a big guy but I was fast.

I gave him a smile before high-tailing it out of the cafe, like I was stealing a piece of artwork, making a run for the getaway car.

———

Thank you for reading Stealth: Mason.

I hope you loved reading about Ariella, Jaxson, and the Eagle Tactical team. Their story continues in CONCEAL: LINCOLN!

I can't tell her she's under my protection...

I've been employed as a bodyguard in the past with Eagle Tactical for celebrities, musicians, even billionaires. I've never had any of them evade my protection.

The little vixen who stormed into my life ended up as my responsibility.

I've been hired to protect her... in secret.

The studio contract is clear. I am not allowed to divulge to her that I'm her personal bodyguard when she leaves the set.

She will find out the truth and when she does, she will hate me.

One-click CONCEAL: LINCOLN now!

And sign up for my newsletter to find out about new books, giveaways, and freebies: www. authorwillowfox.com/subscribe

I appreciate your help in spreading the word, including telling a friend. Reviews help readers find books! Please leave a review on your favorite book site.

GIVEAWAYS, FREE BOOKS, AND MORE GOODIES!

I hope you enjoyed STEALTH and will continue the journey with Jaxson, Ariella, and the Eagle Tactical team.

While this is my first series as Willow Fox, I've been published professionally since 2013.

Sign up for my Willow Fox newsletter

If you enjoyed STEALTH, please take a moment to leave a review. Reviews helps other readers discover my books.

Not sure what to write? That's okay. It doesn't have to be long. You can share how you discovered my book; was it a recommendation by a friend or a book club?

Let readers know who your favorite character is or what you'd like to see happen next. Do you normally read HEA? How are you feeling about the HFN? (I hope satisfied but I promise I will be delivering a HEA at the end of the series!)

Thank you for reading! I hope you'll consider joining my mailing list for free books, promotions, giveaways, and new release news.

ABOUT THE AUTHOR

Willow Fox has loved writing since she was in high school (many ages ago). Her small town romances are reflective of living in a small town in rural America.

Whether she's writing romance or sitting outside by the bonfire reading a good book, Willow loves the magic of the written word.

She dreams of being swept off her feet and hopes to do that to her readers!

Visit her website at:

https://authorwillowfox.com

ALSO BY WILLOW FOX

Eagle Tactical Series

Expose: Jaxson

Stealth: Mason

Conceal: Lincoln

Covert: Jayden

Mafia Marriages

Secret Vow

Captive Vow

Savage Vow

Unwilling Vow

Ruthless Vow

Bratva Brothers

Brutal Boss

Wicked Boss

Possessive Boss

Obsessive Boss

Boxsets

Eagle Tactical Collection

Looking for kinkier books? Try these spicy stories written under the name Allison West.

Boxsets

Academy of Littles

Western Daddies Collection

Obey Daddy Collection

The Alpha Collection

Western Daddies

Her Billionaire Daddy

Her Cowboy Daddy

Her Outlaw Daddy

Her Forbidden Daddy

Standalone Romances

The Victorian Shift

Jailed Little Jade

Prefer a sweeter romance with action and adventure? Check out these titles under the name Ruth Silver.

Aberrant Series

Love Forbidden

Secrets Forbidden

Magic Forbidden

Escape Forbidden

Refuge Forbidden

Boxsets

Gem Apocalypse

Nightblood

Royal Reaper

Royal Deception

Standalones

Stolen Art

www.ingramcontent.com/pod-product-compliance
Lightning Source LLC
Chambersburg PA
CBHW020941030726
47496CB00005B/1289